m/3

Witness to the Future

Other books by Klaus Rifbjerg in English:

Anna (I) Anna (Curbstone Press)
Selected Poems (Curbstone Press)

Klaus Rifbjerg

Witness to the Future

Translated from
the Danish by
Steve Murray

Fjord Press
Seattle
1987

This translation is dedicated to my mother,
Verna F. Murray

Title of Danish edition: *De hellige aber*
Originally published in 1981 by Gyldendal, Copenhagen

Published and distributed by:
Fjord Press
P.O. Box 16501
Seattle, Washington 98116
(206) 625-9363

Editor: Tiina Nunnally
Design & typography: Fjord Press Typography, Seattle
Cover design: Art Chantry Design, Seattle
Author photograph: Steve Murray

Library of Congress Cataloging-in-Publication Data:

Rifbjerg, Klaus.
   Witness to the future.

   Translation of: De hellige aber.
   I. Title.
PT8176.28.I32H4513 1987   839.8'1374   87-17359
ISBN 0-940242-21-4 (alk. paper)
ISBN 0-940242-18-4 (pbk. : alk. paper)

Printed in the United States of America
by Edwards Brothers, Inc.
First edition

Witness to the Future

1

Once there was a boy who found something that nobody else knew about. It was many years ago, so long ago that people who were born just a few years later have absolutely no way of knowing what that time was like. It's as if it never existed at all, even though it was real enough. That's what the boy thought, at least. His name was Mik, or Mikkel. He wore short pants, and every morning when he got up he knew that there was a war going on in Denmark and that there was no chance of it ever stopping. He ate his oatmeal with milk, and even though sugar was rationed he sprinkled on a thick layer because it tasted so good; the sugar crunched between his teeth if he didn't let the milk dissolve it. In between bites he would put his spoon down on the edge of the bowl and sit a while with his hands on his knees. He didn't have to look at them to know how tan they were, and he also knew that if he pulled up his pantlegs a little, his thighs would be whiter than his knees because they weren't sticking out in the sun all day. He enjoyed that difference, the way he got a warm feeling whenever he thought about the place he had found, the one nobody else knew about.

In the evening when he went to bed he thought about the place — about the place and about a lot of other things that belonged to him alone. In the daytime he watched the enemy airplanes flying low over his house, and in the evening before he went to sleep he pretended he was sitting in a plane with different markings on it, shooting down the enemy planes. He was totally calm when he sat in the cockpit maneuvering the airplane; he barely moved his head at all, only glancing down when the enemy plane went into a tailspin below him and vanished into the depths leaving a trail of black smoke. Inside him a great calm spread out in all directions, almost enveloping him and making him feel lightheaded. He was lifted up, floating all by himself, with no airplane at all, and he felt like laughing and crying at the same time.

The place he had found, the one nobody else knew about, didn't give him the same feeling. Just thinking about it made his head swim, of course, but sometimes he would sit up suddenly and stare out into the tenuous darkness, because he wasn't completely sure what he had found, what it meant, or what it could be used for. He was happy about his secret and knew in his heart that he would never reveal it to anyone, not even to his father and mother. Sometimes he wondered whether he ought to tell his big sister about the place, but he was afraid she would laugh at him, so he gave up the idea. On the other hand, Mik was certain that one day, when he had figured out what the place actually was, he would tell his friend Niels about it. He couldn't imagine doing anything if Niels wasn't along. Naturally Niels would kid him about it too, but when Mik showed him the place he would be so surprised — and maybe scared — that he'd forget about teasing him. Mik was sure of that.

A grasshopper chirped in the grass outside the window. Mik lay in bed with his eyes open, trying to imagine how the line looked that separated the two feelings inside him, warmth and uncertainty. He couldn't picture the line, but he still felt it had something to do with the place, which he started thinking about again.

It was entirely by accident that he had stumbled upon the place. Every day he rode his bike around in the hedgerows, either alone or with Niels. One of his favorite spots was an old ruin that lay among tall pine trees and was overgrown with green vines. Once knights or monks had lived there, but now there was only a blackbird and maybe a couple of mice. When the sun was shining the big red stones would warm up, and even when it disappeared the heat from the stones would warm his thighs. Once in a while Mik would climb up in one of the tall pines (even though his parents told him he shouldn't) and sit there looking down on the ruin. But he didn't spot the place from that high vantage point. When he sat on that branch he would often feel sad, because from up there the world seemed completely unalterable. He heard the wind in the branches and felt the big tree sway. He could see the stones of the ruin among the vines. A little farther away the blackbird was singing. It was almost as if everything were coming to a standstill — or had already stopped. Mik didn't know why he felt like crying, but he could feel a weight on his chest. He took a deep breath and sighed.

One day he had been sitting up in the tree feeling utterly miserable. He climbed down because he had gotten cold, and he sat on one of the big stones that were still warm. The sun was gone, and the shadows, gray and transparent, moved in the wind among the green plants. He should have left for home by now, because they were going to eat lunch soon, and his father and mother insisted that he show up on time. He just couldn't get his feet moving, though, and the thought of the bike ride along the sandy paths was unpleasant. He wanted to do something, but he didn't know what, and precisely because he couldn't figure out what he felt like doing, he started to pick at a scab just below his knee. His parents didn't like him to do that either. "You have to leave a scab alone until it falls off, otherwise the sore won't heal," said his father. But Mik still couldn't keep his fingers off it; when he wiggled his fingernail under the edge of the scab it seemed sort of like he was doing something he felt like doing — but he wasn't really sure.

He sat on the warm stone among the green plants, working on his scab so that it wasn't completely attached but hadn't fallen off yet either. That was when he heard the voices for the first time. At first he thought it was the wind in the tall pines — the wind often sounded like it was sighing and moaning at the same time — but then he listened closely, and there was no doubt that somebody was talking. One time with Niels, Mik had surprised a soldier in a gray field uniform who was lying behind some bushes with a girl. Maybe he would be that lucky again. But the sounds were different, and it wasn't only two people talking. It sounded more like a chorus or a whole crowd of people in a marketplace. It couldn't possibly be the mice, even though the sound seemed to come from somewhere between the stones, maybe even right out from under Mik's legs, right where he was sitting. He straightened up and started looking around. The scab on the sore below his knee was still there, but with a moist red border where his fingernail had pried it up.

It was a strange moment. He knew exactly where he was, because he had been there hundreds of times before, and nothing had changed, except for the voices. He also knew that there was a war going on, and that maybe it would end some day, even though that was impossible to imagine. In a way it would have been nice if Niels were there. On the other hand, Mik's head was buzzing because he could hear something no one else had heard. He was quite sure of that. Nobody had heard those voices, or it would have been in the paper.

He started to look around, trying to find out where the voices were coming from. He jumped down from the stone and listened in every direction. The weird thing about the voices was that, although there were a lot of them and they formed a chorus, they still sounded muffled, as though they were coming from under a lid. So they had to be coming from between the stones, maybe through a crack somewhere. But if there weren't any stones the voices would be louder and clearer, so he could hear what they were saying.

Restlessly, Mik ran back and forth, listening to the talking stones. Near a crack at the corner, where the huge blocks met and formed an angle, it seemed to him that the sound grew louder. He tried placing his ear to the crack and heard more clearly now that it wasn't only voices coming out of it, but other sounds as well: roaring, a kind of thunder, whining, moaning, and crashes without end that kept expanding into clouds of sound and really couldn't be described at all; they reminded him of something up in heaven he didn't understand. Suddenly he felt an urge to run. Although the ruin had been exciting enough before because knights or monks had once lived there, all of a sudden it became foreign and threatening. It wasn't Niels and Mik's ruin anymore. But then Mik realized that the ruin was much more his than Niels'. That's why he was still standing there instead of running off to his bicycle and riding home.

For three days he worked with a big rock and an old chisel he had found over at Jens Ewald's. He hammered and pounded as he listened to the sounds growing stronger every day. Finally the opening was big enough for him to squeeze in feet first and jackknife the rest of his body through. Now there was no lid on the sounds anymore. They roared all around him so that he had to cover his ears; it was almost as if he could feel the pressure of the wind, and the sounds had turned into a mighty draft rushing and flowing toward the new opening he himself had made. The effort of squeezing in through the crack and the transition from the bright light outside to the darkness in the chamber made him squint his eyes. Then he stood there a while like the three monkeys on the chiffonier in their house in the city, not speaking, not hearing, not seeing. A little later, though, he opened his eyes and took his hands away from his ears, and now he discovered — after he had gotten used to the semi-darkness — that he was standing in a kind of cave. The crack had been narrow, so maybe that's why the room seemed larger. He shivered at the feeling of the clammy draft, which seemed powerful because it wasn't just a damp wind, but waves of sound, a sausage-shaped stream that whooshed past his body and head and struck his eardrums at the same time. The light through the cracks in the ramparts cast patterns on the dim walls, and Mik noticed that water was dripping from the ceiling over the many jagged projections. He knew that he had gotten inside the ruin, but the space didn't look like a hall. At least he couldn't imagine the monks walking around in here, or the knights. It was more a place for turtles and toads, if anything living could survive here. He was afraid he wouldn't be able to stay alive in here very long either, but then he heard the sounds again; they didn't exactly make the cave pleasant, but they did seem to come from somebody, or something associated with people.

Unable to decide what he really wanted to do — whether to investigate where the sounds were coming from and what they meant, or to rush out into the daylight, home to everything familiar — he stood listening to his heart. He had only done that before when he was sick and had a fever, and his heart became alive and strange, an independent part of him. That's how it felt now, and for a moment he thought that since he only had one heart and would never get another one, maybe it was a good idea to listen to its signals. What was his heart saying? It was beating faster than usual; in fact it was pounding all the way up in his throat and sending a murmuring rhythm all around his navel. He thought he was still scared, but at the same time his heart kept saying, "Look, look, look!" and he felt how warm the current was flowing inside him, so he began to take small steps forward, into the darkness of the cave and away from the cracks in the wall behind him.

With every step Mik took, the cave widened. The walls diverged from him and the ceiling lifted as though all of a sudden it had become a cloud or the sky itself. He expected to see stars any minute now. The light behind him had vanished completely. Then he felt his heart again, and this time it sounded an alarm! He would never get out of here, because now it was pitch dark, and all he had left behind flared up in him like a huge torch. He thought of his father and his mother and his big sister, who were probably already searching for him and calling his name. In his mind he saw his bed and the whitewashed window frame, and he could hear the sound of the hasp banging when the wind blew and the window was ajar. He could taste the oatmeal and milk and sugar. He could see the roast pork on the serving plate in the evening and the bowl of parsley sauce next to it. He thought of Niels' white ankle socks with the blue border. He remembered all their games. But just as he was about to start crying and lie down on the cold, damp stones and give up, he heard the flowing sound and felt that he had to find out where it came from and what it meant, because otherwise nothing had any meaning at all, and he might as well lie down and die. He closed his eyes and held his hands over his ears, pressing his lips together. For a moment he had to be the three monkeys from home again, who didn't see or hear or speak, and as he stood like that he heard the sound of his own heart even louder, while the great noise he had been following the whole time disappeared. Beating more slowly and strongly now, his heart pumped thoughts into his brain, and when he had pulled himself together he turned around and walked in the direction he thought he had come from. He knew he hadn't gone around any corners. The room had just expanded and had gotten darker and darker. After a while he noticed that it started to narrow again, and when he opened his eyes he caught a faint glimpse of the light from the cracks in the wall and the hole he had chiseled himself, where a bluish glow ringed by gold showed the way out.

He squeezed himself through the hole so eagerly he didn't notice that the sharp edge of a broken stone scraped the scab off the little sore below his knee. When he stood outside and saw that everything was the same as before — the green vines, the tall, sighing trees, the sun moving between scudding clouds — he completely forgot to listen to his heart and barely remembered how scared he had been a minute ago.

Still, he couldn't resist turning around and staring at the crack that led into the cave. When he had stared at it for a while, he leaned over and put his ear to it. The sounds were still there, but more muted than when they had engulfed him completely. He could feel their whooshing and whistling against his ear like a draft, and while he stood like that it was as though the sounds not only reached his eardrums, but also found their way into his ear and farther in, to his brain, and all the way down into his heart. He had escaped, but he also knew that he had to go back again. Carefully he gathered up some of the shards of rock he had chipped off and stuffed them into the hole. When he was finished, he sealed the cracks with moss and dirt, because there was a war on, and he knew how to camouflage things so other people couldn't see them.

Then he rode home with his secret, but instead of returning the chisel he had found at Jens Ewald's house, he kept it and hid it behind the firewood in the woodshed of the summer house, because he might have use for it later.

2

For several days Mikkel avoided thinking about the place no one else knew about. At least he didn't think about it during the day; he only brought out the memory in the evening, letting the sights and sounds pour over him. When he lay in bed after his mother had said goodnight, he quietly tried to approach the line separating him from the image of what he had experienced. He shut his eyes halfway and felt himself getting closer and closer. If he didn't do it too fast he could slow down and postpone the moment a little longer. It was like being a rubber band that was stretched tighter and tighter, but never to the breaking point. Then he let go and the picture of the ruin and the crack between the stones loomed up. In his mind he could see the place the way it was when he squeezed into the cave, but also the way he had left it, hidden. At least he hoped it was hidden; it would be a catastrophe if anyone else found it. It was his place, he was the one who found it, it belonged to him.

After a while he calmed down again. Almost nobody went to the ruin, and the people that sometimes drank their Sunday coffee among the stones and the green vines saw nothing but what was there. They were like his own father and mother and Niels' father and mother. They only saw what was there.

One night the images and the sounds kept on haunting him so he hardly slept a wink. He knew that he had to go back to the place and in through the crack. He had thought of taking his kite string along so he could find his way back to the entrance of the cave, but other than that he didn't know what he was going to do. Several times during the night he had thought of Niels; when he went out to pee in the grass beside the pump and looked at the stars shining over his head by the thousands, he decided to initiate his friend into his secret. He just couldn't keep it all to himself, and he also knew that if he had to go into the darkness he would have to have someone along, otherwise he would never get out again.

While he was eating his breakfast his mother asked him if he was sick. He looked so pale. But he smiled at her and said there was nothing wrong. He knew why he was pale, and as he lifted his spoon to his mouth and let the mixture of oatmeal and milk and sugar swish around, he couldn't help smiling a little because he knew something she didn't. She walked back and forth like she always did, set things out or put them back on the shelf. She was the same shape she had always been, a warm figure that bent over his bed when he was very small, picked him up, and carried him around; or now, giving him food, asking him how he was, telling him what he could and couldn't do, putting him to bed at night, tucking his comforter around him and wishing him good-night. He loved her.

But now he had discovered something he had absolutely no desire to tell her about. It was strange, but he felt that way about his mother and father and his big sister too, even though at one time he had wanted to tell her about it. He didn't know why, but they were outside of it somehow — even his big sister, although she was closer in a way. They would laugh or shake their heads or say that he mustn't play in the ruin. Or maybe they wouldn't even listen to what he was saying. He told so many stories, after all.

With Niels it was different. Of course there was no doubt that he would have to be convinced in the beginning too, but that didn't matter so much. When he realized what Mik had found he would be impressed anyway.

After breakfast Mik got up, put his bowl in the sink, and turned on the faucet, letting the water run into the bowl. Milk and the few remaining bits of oatmeal flowed over the edge, and a moment later the bowl looked clean. He shut off the water and told his mother he was going out. She nodded and said that they were eating lunch at noon. For a moment he thought about the lunch hour and visualized it quite clearly: the hands of the clock pointing straight up and covering each other, his father going to sit at the head of the table, his sister to the right of him, his mother walking back and forth, and Mik himself at the other end of the table.

In the summertime his father got up late and sometimes stretched breakfast out almost all the way to lunchtime. That was part of summer, and they didn't go to the beach until afternoon because it was a long way. Mik pictured it all and then thought of the table without him, of the beach without him there, and for a moment he hesitated on the doorstep. Then he hurried down the little path through the high grass, disappeared in between the pine trees, skirted Henrik Jensen's house, crossed the narrow bridge with the railing over the ditch, and hopped over the wheel ruts and the gate to Niels' house.

Niels had gotten up and was sitting on the doorstep in the sun. The light was shining brightly on his brown hair curling in every direction. Inside each curl there was a deep shadow, and when he raised his head and looked at Mik, for an instant it looked like snakes winding all over his head. He squinted in the sunlight and smiled slightly, and Mik thought briefly of the picture of the faun he had seen in a book.

It was harder than he had thought to tell Niels about the place. He got up the nerve several times but didn't know quite how to begin. What should he say? That there was a secret cave in the ruin? That he had heard voices, sounds, whooshing, thundering? If only it were just something he had dreamed. They talked about all sorts of other things, but the conversation lagged because it was one of those days when Niels was being difficult. He demanded one suggestion after another, but he rejected them just as fast as they were made. Mik wondered for a moment whether he should leave. But then he thought about the darkness in the cave and the power of the sounds, and since he was angry about Niels' contrariness at the same time, he suddenly spit out the whole story. It came tumbling out of him lickety-split; at first, of course, it was as if Niels hadn't heard anything at all, but at last he said something.

"Oh, I know you and your stories."

Mik didn't say a word. His face was flushed and his throat was dry, he had talked so much.

"A cup of blood or seven holes in your head," Niels said.

Mik snorted. That crap, that was an old story. He had asked Niels what he would rather do: get seven holes in his head or drink a cup of blood. Maybe he had also told him that he drank a cup of blood every morning himself. He told so many stories. You had to tell a lot of stories. But now that he was trying to explain something real, he wanted to be believed, even though it sounded incredible.

Again he felt the urge to get up and leave. He felt alone and a little sad. He looked up into the clear air and saw the swallows flying back and forth. He heard the insects buzzing too, and from the trees and the flowers came a powerful aroma that drew his senses out toward other sights and smells: the yellow color of summer butter, the black abdomen of the scabiosa moth and the red spots on its wings, the aromatic roughness of wild strawberries on his tongue, the sweet clump of cream at the top of the Jersey milk bottle, the rustling of quaking-grass, the profusion of flowers along the edge of ditches, the smell of a down comforter after it had been aired out in the sunshine. He felt sad because he was on his way toward a dividing line again, in fact he felt as if he always stood at a point of transition, something he had to pass through, something he was supposed to prove and make others believe and take part in. It was difficult, almost impossible. Mik wondered why, but this time he wasn't going to give up. What he had found was just too exciting, and he knew he couldn't conquer it without Niels. He needed his friend.

"Why are you such a moron?" he asked.

Niels was sitting throwing his knife into the ground as though he were playing splits.

"You're the one who's a moron."

"Yeah, but why won't you believe me? All you have to do is come with me and see for yourself."

"Voices and whooshing and roaring in the ruin . . . ha!"

At that moment Niels' mother came out the door to the porch. She raised her hand to shade her eyes from the sunlight, and the brim of her straw sun hat was bent back slightly. She had a cigarette in the corner of her mouth, and she was wearing a white dress.

"Hi, Mikkel," she said. "What a nice sunny day."

She looked down at him and smiled. Mik thought she was beautiful, but in a different way than his mother was. In a little while she would go back in the house, and then she probably wouldn't come out for a long time.

Niels stood up. "We're going for a walk," he said.

"Where are you going?"

"Down to the ruin. Mik says . . ."

He caught himself and shrugged his shoulders. Mik's face had turned red. The two boys looked at each other. Then Niels smiled and squinted.

"You know what time we're eating," said his mother.

"Yeah, I know."

The two boys stood there a moment in taut anticipation,

then they started to run, and it was as if they were running in every direction at once, even though they were really heading for Mikkel's house the whole time. But first Niels had to get his bike, and Mik remembered the kite string and the chisel, which it was essential to take along. He also wondered whether he should get his windbreaker, and he told Niels that they had better take along some extra clothes because it was cold and damp inside. And matches. Niels shook his head; neither of them was allowed to carry matches, but still he stuck his hand through the open window to his big brother's room and snatched a box of them lying on the table.

By the time they rode through the hedge surrounding the ruin they had windbreakers, matches, an extra sweater, a bottle of milk, and ten lumps of stolen sugar with them, plus the chisel and kite string. But the best of all was Niels' flashlight, which he remembered at the last minute. He seemed to believe that what Mik had told him was true. When they had almost reached the ruin, Mik was suddenly afraid that maybe the whole thing was only something he had dreamed. He slowed down his bike, but when he saw Niels lie flat over his handlebars and zoom into the last curve on the sandy path before the big pine trees, he pushed down hard on the pedals to get there at the same time as his friend.

Their bikes lay in the grass with their back wheels spinning, they jumped off them so fast. Then it occurred to Mik that they had better lock them if they were going to stay very long in the cave. Niels shrugged, and they went back to the bikes. While he was squatting and locking the bike with his key, Mik took a good look around. There shouldn't be anyone around, and as far as he could see, there wasn't. The big

pine trees sighed in the wind as usual, and the blackbird was
singing in the bushes over by the gravel pit. Niels stood with
his windbreaker over his shoulder and waited.

"What are you doing?" he asked.

"Nothing."

"Then why aren't you coming? Is it because you're
scared?"

Mik stood up.

"Of course you made it all up anyway," said Niels, "just
like everything else."

The blackbird whistled, and Mik felt as if he couldn't
move at all. He had no doubt that the cave was in the same
spot it was before. Still he felt strangely helpless without
being able to say why. Maybe he suddenly remembered how
scared he had been in there last time and how much he had
longed for the summer house and his family, or maybe he was
experiencing again how complicated things could be, both
around him and inside himself. When it came right down to
it, he didn't know what was waiting for him behind the warm
red blocks of stone either. The voices and the sounds—what
were they? Of course, there was a war going on, and the black
airplanes came every day and shot over their heads at a target
down on the beach. But that was only in the morning. Otherwise it was very quiet, and the sun shone; unless it was rain-
ing, with drops hanging underneath the leaves of the orpine
on the roof, where moss and heather also grew. It was quiet
and peaceful; they were in the country, where the air tasted
fresh and good and nothing ever changed. As long as he could
remember, things had been the same. But wasn't that just

what he found so oppressive? The fact that nothing changed, that everything was always the same?

He looked at Niels again, started walking, and said, "Come on."

With his hands on his hips like some kind of expert, Mik assumed a stance and scanned the corner of the ruin where he knew the cave should be. He squinted and tilted his head to one side, then took a couple of steps forward and started scratching in the shards and the solidified dirt between the cracks. A little later he found the opening and put his ear to it. A damp wind reached his eardrum, and the sounds were like they were the day he found the cave: whistling, rumbling, screaming, wailing, moaning, roaring, but not as individual sounds that could be distinguished one by one — it was a long, flowing noise like a sausage that would never end. Mik beckoned to Niels. A moment later his friend stood beside him.

"Listen for yourself," said Mik.

Niels glanced at him with raised eyebrows, then went over to the crack Mik was pointing at and pressed his ear to it. He raised his head and looked at Mik, then he listened again.

"What is it?" he asked.

Mik shook his head.

"It sounds like . . . everything."

The curls in Niels' hair shook a little when he moved his head back and forth to be able to hear better. The snakes writhed. Then he straightened up.

"It's just the wind . . . from inside."

Mik handed him the chisel. "Take the rocks out."

Niels stared at the tool for a second, then got started. He braced his knee against the stones underneath and set to work. Mik went over and bent down next to him, and in a moment the opening was quite visible, and the sounds flowed out louder than before, while the dampness increased. They used to talk about digging all the way to China, but that was when they were smaller; this was something else. Mik looked over his shoulder. If anyone came the whole thing would be ruined. He glanced at Niels and knew that now he believed him, or at least he believed more than he did before. And now they were going to go into the cave together. If they wanted to avoid being discovered, they would have to close it behind them, and it was also necessary to fasten the kite string to something so they could be sure of finding their way back and not getting lost. After all, both of them had promised to be home for lunch.

Mik crawled through the narrow opening first. It was his cave, after all, but Niels followed along a moment later, and then they stood side by side in the darkness Mik had experienced by himself three days earlier. He had the ball of kite string in his hand, and when they had collected themselves a bit he got down on his knees, placed the string on the floor of the cave, and started scraping rocks toward him from outside so that the opening got very small and there was a chance that nobody would notice anything peculiar if they decided to go into the ruin. With Niels' help he got one end of the kite string fastened under one of the big blocks of stone by the entrance, and then they both turned and started walking into the darkness in the direction the sounds seemed to be coming from, while they held onto the ball and let the string pay out behind them. The darkness grew deeper, the dampness increased, but the sound did too. Soon Niels stopped and turned to Mik. The whites of his eyes gleamed.

"The flashlight," he said. "We forgot the flashlight!"

Mik felt inside his windbreaker. There it was. They hadn't forgotten it; neither of them had thought of it until now. He unbuttoned his pocket, fished out the flashlight, and turned it on. He let the light play over the walls of the cave overhead; it all looked the same as before. There was water everywhere, dripping and trickling, and when he moved the light a little farther down, Mik also thought he saw something scurry across the floor. It had to be a mouse. He had seen them before up in the daylight, and for a moment he thought of the blackbird that used to whistle when he played in the ruin. He couldn't hear it anymore. He felt like going back, but now Niels was with him, so it was harder — unless Niels had had enough too. Mik glanced at him. He couldn't tell what his friend was thinking. His expression was inscrutable; he looked like he was concentrating, trying to figure out what was actually happening, and where they were heading. He knew the secret now; Mik wasn't the only one anymore. That helped them stick together but also made it hard to talk about everything. They had to feel their way along with each other, the way Mik had the impression that grownups did. But there was no danger, of course, there was nothing really to be afraid of; in his hand he had the string and the stick it was wrapped around, and they could go back to where they started in minutes. Except for the cave, which was exciting enough, they hadn't seen everything yet and hadn't figured out what the sounds were at all, or where they came from. He poked Niels with his elbow, and they started forward again.

Soon they were out in the large room where Mik had been by himself. The sounds now seemed to come from every direction; they boomed and echoed under the vaulted ceiling. But when they listened closely it seemed as though the noise had a definite source. Mik let the beam of light play up and down over the huge walls that climbed high toward the darkness and vanished in an impenetrable gloom. It occurred to him that they must be inside a mountain, but he had never seen a mountain, either from the outside or the inside, and there weren't any mountains in Denmark. So they must have gone down without having noticed it, and maybe they were really on their way to China — or to the bowels of the earth. He shivered.

"I'm a little scared," he said.

Niels looked at him.

"Me too."

Joy rushed through Mik. It was the first time he had heard his friend say that he was scared. That never would have happened on the other side of the hole in the ruin. But now he said it, and Mik was just about to reach out and grab Niels' hand, but stopped himself; they weren't so little that they could go around holding hands, after all.

"Should we turn back?"

Niels shook his head.

"No, we have to find out about it . . . about the sounds, so we can go back. I think it's a factory. Maybe it's a secret factory where they make weapons."

"Yeah, but then it would be forbidden to come in here."

"There's probably a sign. There are always signs if something is forbidden."

Mik nodded. Up on the surface they had both seen signs that said "No Trespassing — Military Area." There were lots of them. But right now there was only the dark and the damp and the weird stream of noise that almost reminded them of big, whirring wheels but was still different somehow, more complicated, whimpering and whining, as if someone were trying to scream but couldn't quite get it out.

Niels had started moving forward again, and Mik had to sweep the flashlight beam to find him. When the light struck Niels, Mik saw his friend's shadow loom up the rock wall. For an instant he felt more terrified than ever before, but it was mostly because he was reminded of all those ghost stories Niels and his big brother knew, and the times when Niels had ambushed him at night, sticking out his grinning face lit from below with a flashlight. It was essential not to be afraid now, though it didn't matter as long as they were both equally scared. He hurried over to his friend and stood next to him. The shadow shrank, and Mik discovered that they couldn't go any farther unless they started following along the wall. The question now was whether they should go to the left or to the right. They tried to orient themselves by the sound, and soon they agreed that it was coming more strongly from the right.

With their left hands feeling along the rock wall they fumbled their way forward. Now and then they stumbled over rocks and large boulders that had fallen out of the darkness, and when Mik shone his light around, it was as though the light disappeared, didn't strike anything, and was swallowed up. The sound, on the other hand, got louder, and there seemed to be a change in the temperature. It got warmer, and at the same time the smell was different, more acrid, puckering and prickling their skin. Several times the rock wall changed direction, but they weren't thinking about it anymore, not even when the wall on the opposite side came closer and the cave seemed to constrict and turn into a kind of tunnel. Only when Mik felt a tug in his hand and discovered that the kite string had run out did he stop and feel the cold creeping up and down the collar of his windbreaker. He grabbed Niels' sleeve and stopped him.

"There's no more string. We'll have to turn back."

Niels turned his head and stared at him.

"No more string . . . but we're almost there!"

"Almost there?"

"Yes, can't you feel it? The sounds have gotten much louder, and it's warm here, and it smells. Can't you feel it?"

"Sure. But it smells *bad*."

"We can't turn back now."

"Yeah, but the string . . ."

Niels scratched his head through all his thick hair.

"If you wait here, then you can yell when I've gone a little farther — and found out what it is."

"What if you don't find out what it is?"

"Then I'll come back."

Mik felt that the cave didn't belong to him at all anymore. This was how it usually went; if he suggested something, then Niels would quickly take it over as his own. He hung his head and felt abandoned.

"But what if . . . what if this is hell?" he said.

As soon as he said it he knew he'd made a mistake, and Niels shot back at him: "Aw, what a bunch of crap. Hell! There isn't any hell, that's what my dad says."

Mik's father said basically the same thing, even though they seldom talked about either heaven or hell. The kite-string stick was clammy in his hand, and he felt the string tighten because there was no more slack.

Then he heard Niels shout: "Look, look over there, there's a light!"

Mik squinted and stared straight ahead. At first he couldn't see anything, but then he noticed a weak glow, a little glimmer of something red and yellowish that danced up and down on the opposite wall about ten yards farther down the tunnel.

"Can't you see it? There's a light!"

All of a sudden there was a violent gust of heat and light and stench. His throat felt like it was knotting up, and Mik involuntarily put his hand to his throat and clamped the collar of his windbreaker in against his skin. He closed his eyes too, and when he opened them again he saw that Niels had started walking forward and was disappearing faster and faster down toward the flickering light, which also seemed to be getting brighter.

"Niels," he shouted, "Niels, don't go!"

But his friend kept on going; he didn't stop or turn around until he was all the way down by the light. His face was no more than a white dot, but it was suddenly restless, dancing with shadows like living ribbons up over his eyebrows and cheekbones. At the same time he was pointing in a new direction — where the light was evidently streaming from — and shouting: "Come on . . . come on and look!"

His voice echoed, and among the other sounds the sound of Niels' voice bounced off the ceiling and the walls of the cave: "Look, look, look," it said.

Mik didn't know what to do. He was standing with the kite string in his hand, and there wasn't any more left. If they ever wanted to find their way back to the ruin, they wouldn't make it without the string. It just wouldn't work. But at the same time Niels was standing there shouting, and Mik knew that the point of the whole trip, the point of everything he had found, was down there where the light and the sounds were coming from.

Then he heard Niels' voice again: "You've got to come — we're there!"

Mik was shaking all over. Now there was no doubt that he had reached the dividing line. The rubber band was stretched to the breaking point. When he let go of the stick with the kite string he would be letting go of *everything*.

But Niels kept shouting: "It's right here. We can find our way back. Just put down the string. Come on. Come and look!"

With a trembling heart Mik put down the stick. He felt the little knot where the string was wrapped around the branch, and for a moment he pushed his finger against a knot in the wood and remembered that it was an ash twig he had cut with his own knife. Thank goodness the knife was in his belt; it wasn't big, but it had a groove on the blade and was very sharp and pointed and a little curved. He could clearly picture the house and the yard around it with the broom bushes and the small birch trees, but he pushed the images away, because at that instant a new, enormous feeling streamed over him. He was himself. He was doing something he had never tried before, he was alone — except for Niels — and he was on his way to something . . . something different that was entirely his own.

When he let go of the kite-string stick and laid it on the floor of the tunnel, it jumped back a little toward the darkness where they had come from. It was as if someone had pulled on the other end, but Mik knew that he had just been holding the string so taut that it had to contract a little when he let it go. For a moment he stared down at the stick and shone the flashlight beam on it; then he started walking toward Niels and soon was standing next to him. The light was still smoldering across his friend's face, making it undulate and change expression so that Mik couldn't tell if he was laughing or crying or terrified. But he followed his gaze, and there, where the tunnel bent and continued in another direction, he saw at the end something that looked like the entrance to a furnace, a big hole where light and sound glowed and radiated in all directions, grew stronger and weaker, changed color — alive like the sun and the stars and the fireballs in a gigantic fireworks display. He opened his eyes wide and took a deep breath, but then he squeezed his eyes shut and held his hands over his ears and stood like that until he felt Niels' hand on his arm and heard his voice.

"That's the entrance."

"The entrance?"

"Yes. Or the exit."

"But . . . it's all on fire," Mik said.

"No, no, it's not on fire. It's just . . . oh, I don't know. I don't think it's burning."

Mik opened his eyes all the way. It was still warm, and there was a strong, bitter smell, but there wasn't any fire. The shifting colors were evidently not burning—though they weren't cold either. It was a little like looking at a star, but they were always so far away. Here the star was very close. If it was a star.

Mik didn't know what it was he saw; how could he? If his father or mother had been there, or even his big sister, they would certainly have known what it was. But they were far away—very far away, he thought suddenly. And it was no use wondering about them either, because it was unthinkable that they would be able to stand here with him. They would never have crawled into the cave, they would simply never have believed it existed, and if he had told them about it they would have said that he should stay away from it, or that it was just a bunch of nonsense.

He glanced back at Niels, whose eyes were wide. The light from the furnace door played over his entire face, and on top of his head the snakelike curls were writhing in every possible color.

"Do you dare?" asked Mik.

"Dare what?"

"Go down there," Mik pointed.

Niels shrugged his shoulders. "Oh, I don't know," he said. "Do you?"

"I don't know. Don't you think we'll burn up?"

Niels seemed annoyed. "I told you already, we won't get burned. They're cold flames, can't you feel it yourself?"

"But the smell . . . and the heat. It smells horrible here!"

"You probably still think it's hell," Niels taunted him.

"I never said that."

"No, but that's what you think. You believe in hell. And you're the one with 'seven holes in your head and a cup of blood.' You're the one that drinks a cup of blood every day!"

Mik didn't say a word. He was staring at the swirling hole of light and sound and stench. In his whole life he had never seen anything like it, and he was scared, but he couldn't figure out how scared he ought to be. In a way, it was creepier inside the cave in the dark; on the other hand, there was good reason to be really scared, since they didn't know a thing about what it was they were looking at, and what it might do to them.

The war back home was scary enough, maybe, but it wasn't really that bad. Nothing ever happened; it was all just like before. But here was an opportunity — or rather two of them. They could either turn back at once and follow the kite string back to the ruin, or they could go up to the entrance (or exit) and see what happened. Mik heard the sobbing inside him. It wasn't urgent, it was more like an echo of all the times he had cried in his life. He remembered what it was like to cry without thinking about it, and he also remembered how crying had ruled him when he was very small. It sprang forth like a huge bubble deep inside and opened up his whole body. It seemed as though it would never stop, and it continued in hiccups and deep sighs long after the sobs had actually stopped. He wasn't going to cry like that now. He would never cry like a little boy again.

"Come on," he said to Niels, "let's go."

He reached out and took his friend's hand, and they walked like that through the tunnel and the swirling and flaming light.

3

It was like having been asleep or unconscious; when they opened their eyes again they didn't know where they were. The light was normal, and all the flames and shifting rays were gone. The damp heat was gone too, and only the acrid, bitter, pungent, and now somewhat sweetish smell was left. The sound had changed to a constant booming, a rhythmic rumbling, humming, and whistling, broken by deep grunts and coughs. The first thing Mik saw was a road — or what he thought had to be a road, for he had never seen anything like it. Through the hills wound a six-lane cement ribbon as far as the eye could see in both directions, and he saw things driving on it that looked like cars — or what he thought were cars. They looked much different and sounded much different than any of the cars he had seen in his life. Their sound was at once softer and more penetrating than that of normal cars, and they all drove very fast, zooming down the road in both directions, passing each other and going around the trucks, which were much larger and had trailers attached and belched thick, reeking smoke behind them.

Mik noticed that Niels let go of his hand, but he himself didn't move. He kept staring at the strange road and tried to figure out how they had gotten through the hole in the furnace, and where they were. It was a foreign place — yet there was something familiar about it. It was strange, but not completely foreign. He turned his head a little and saw that they were standing in front of a little hill or knoll. It must be a Viking burial mound. His father had shown him some, and Mik was sure that's what it was. They were standing in front of a burial mound. But where it was located and how they had gotten there he did not understand. The landscape was unfamiliar; it wasn't anywhere near the summer house. At least he had never been here before.

Then he noticed that there was a sort of entrance to the burial mound. Or was it an exit? Was that the one they had come out of? They would have to investigate that if they ever wanted to go back. And they had to go back; they had promised to be home for lunch! Mik suddenly got worried because he really didn't know where he was, and even though the countryside reminded him of something he recognized, it was still so foreign and smelled so different that it had to be *a foreign country*. He also thought of the kite string that was now lying in the darkness down there on the other side of the entrance. Would they ever find it again?

While he was worrying about all these things, he looked around and discovered that the burial mound they were standing in front of wasn't the only one. There were many of them; the whole landscape seemed to be full of them, and they all looked the same. The only difference was that some of them had fences around them and others were bare. Mik was really scared.

"Have you noticed?" he asked Niels.

Niels was still standing and staring at the huge road where the cars zoomed into the distance in both directions at tremendous speed.

"What?"

"That there are a lot of burial mounds."

"Sure, but the road," said Niels, "did you see the road? It's gigantic."

Mik nodded. "Yeah, I saw it. Do you know where we are?"

Niels didn't answer. Then he shook his head. "They must be cars. They are cars, they can't be anything else."

"But how are we going to get home?" asked Mik. "Do you know which way we came from?"

Niels looked around. "Nope. Wasn't it from the burial mound?"

"Yeah, but there are a lot of them."

"We'll have to investigate them. But first we have to look . . . we've got to take a look at this over here."

He started to walk down toward the huge cement ribbon where the noise rose and fell but was always constant and thick with overtones like a kind of whining that was hard to believe, or listen to. Suddenly Mik thought that Niels looked ridiculous. The legs of his short pants were very wide and flapped against his thighs with each step; his sandals looked too big for some reason too. He walked down the lumpy grass field like a duck, and as he strode along, his curly hair bounced in the wind, and he smoothed it back with one hand as he turned down the collar of his windbreaker. It was impossible to say why there was suddenly something wrong with his friend's clothes — in fact, Mik was usually jealous of Niels because he thought his clothes were sharper-looking than his own, but right there, just now, something was wrong.

At the thought of how he must look in his Tyrolean suspenders and sneakers (which he had nagged his mother to get for him, even though she said they were bad for him), his face turned red. It was a strange feeling, and he didn't know how to handle it or where it came from. What was it that was wrong? The first time he had stood by a burial mound with his father he had been dressed almost the same way, and nothing had been wrong then. There were burial mounds here too, but still something wasn't quite right. He wanted to yell and tell Niels to wait, but all at once an enormous shadow exploded over his head and rushed at blinding speed over the field, and it had scarcely passed over Niels before a sound that was truly indescribable tossed them both to the ground.

He thought that he had finally been caught by the heat and roar streaming and boiling inside the cave; then Mik saw what had knocked them to the ground. A huge, wedge-shaped object streaked low over the field and the bending river of cement. It had scarcely disappeared before an identical flying contraption followed and once more threatened to burst their heads with noise. The two planes (for they had to be planes) vanished toward the horizon, and out of the tail end of their compact fuselages streamed — besides the deadly noise — thin plumes of black smoke that remained hanging in the air.

The sound took a while to die out, but Mik kept his hands pressed to his ears, and he saw that Niels was doing the same. They cautiously tried sitting up. Pale, they stared at each other; then they noticed that the cars were still driving along the road as though nothing had happened, and that both of them were still alive. Far away, almost invisible, the planes changed course upward and climbed and climbed; they got smaller and smaller, and when they had climbed so high that they could no longer be seen with the naked eye, they were transformed into white stripes and existed only as soundless writing against the blue sky.

Mik crawled over to Niels and sat down next to him. "What was that?"

"I don't know."

"Were they planes?"

"Yeah. Some kind of planes, I think."

"I was scared. More scared than in the cave."

"Nothing happened, though."

"But you thought something would, didn't you?"

"Yeah."

Mik didn't know what else to say. He looked all around; it looked empty, even though they could see the enormous road for several miles to each side. The sound that was no longer there had left an emptiness inside, a kind of vacuum, which was also a fear that the noise would return, sudden and deadly. But now it was quiet, except for the sound of the cars. Mik was still baffled, because he usually felt safe near a road. Whenever he emerged from a path through the hedge and saw an asphalt road, he always knew that he would be able to find his way home. But this road apparently led nowhere. It came out of a void beyond the horizon and vanished into another on the other side of the hills. Where was it going? Where did the cars end up when they finally slowed down and stopped? Even the way the road was laid out with three lanes on each side didn't make sense. A road usually followed the landscape; it curved and disappeared in valleys and went up hills. Here it curved out of sight like a meaningless scar in a landscape where there was nothing but the burial mounds and the fields. Mik sighed and shook his head. He felt like he didn't understand a thing.

Suddenly he realized that there was only the sound of the cars' engines and their tires on the cement since the flying triangles had gone. He squinted and stared up into the bright sunlight. When he turned his head from side to side he saw nothing. There wasn't a bird anywhere! He thought of the blackbird by the ruin, but that wasn't what was missing; blackbirds didn't like open fields. Then he realized that there weren't any swallows. They couldn't have flown south already, it was still too early in the summer. But even above the barley fields where they liked to zigzag back and forth over the long stalks, not a single one could be seen.

He got a funny feeling in his stomach again. He had never consciously thought about swallows before. They had always been there in the summer, after all. Maybe they didn't live here — in China. But were they really in China? Mik hadn't imagined China would be like this. The countryside was foreign and terrifying, all right, but it still reminded him in a strange way of his own. They couldn't be very far from home, he was sure of that. He just didn't know which direction it was, and that was another reason why the feeling of emptiness was overwhelming. He missed the birds. In a way he was obsessed with the thought of them. They should have been there! There also should have been a house with an open Dutch door or a gate where they would fly back and forth, back and forth, all day long. The sound they made was so different from the one he was listening to now, and the one he had heard a moment ago. Even the enemy airplanes that flew over with barking machine guns were not half as frightening as the planes — or whatever they were — they had just seen. Good Lord, the fighter planes were really slow. You could hear them coming and hear them going away. No surprises there. Here the sky suddenly opened up and everything was engulfed and exploded in noise. It was clear: even the birds must have been scared away.

It occurred to him that it wasn't just fear and homesickness turning over in his stomach — he was hungry too. Niels had gotten up and was standing a few feet away staring at the burial mounds. He was frowning. Then he turned toward Mik.

"Where was it we came out?" he asked.

"Over there," said Mik, pointing. "I think it was over there."

Niels pointed at another burial mound. "Wasn't it over there?"

Mik wasn't sure. "I don't know exactly . . ."

Niels shook his head so his curls bounced. "You have to know. It was your idea, and a minute ago . . ." He broke off.

Mik made a great effort. There had been a hole where they came out, he was sure of that. Otherwise they never would have come out. And he had seen it himself. It was a burial mound without a fence, and there had been an entrance — or an exit. Mik got up and started walking back and forth between the burial mounds on top of the hill. All of a sudden they looked exactly alike, even though some had fences and some didn't. But there weren't any with holes in them. He turned to Niels. "What time is it?"

Niels looked at his watch. "Ten minutes to twelve." He looked angry. "And I promised to be home at noon. You heard me say so yourself."

Mik thought about his own lunch. He was supposed to be home too. It was very important that they both get home at the right time. Their parents made a point of it — and how else would they ever get anything to eat?

"We'll have to find the cave."

He ran quickly around one of the burial mounds, but it was completely sealed. There was no entrance anywhere. He thought that even if they found the cave and the kite string and ran and ran all the way and rode as fast as they could on their bikes, they would still get home too late. He had shown up late before, and it wasn't pleasant. He knew that Niels was in the same spot, because their hired girl would hit him. She had explained to Niels that she had to do it, because she was the one who had to answer to his parents; if the boy didn't learn early to obey and do what he was told, he would have trouble the rest of his life. Mik's father and mother didn't talk that way, but his mother would get very sad and not say anything — maybe for several hours — if he had been naughty, and it was unbearable. So they had to try and get home.

"I can't find it," he said to Niels. "I thought it was there before, when we came out. But now I can't find the hole."

Somewhere in his throat the sobs were building. But he wouldn't let them out, he refused, he was too big for that, and he couldn't let his friend see him crying, especially not when he was the one who had thought up the whole thing. So he said instead, "Can't we make a phone call — to Larsen the grocer?"

"A call? Where are you going to call from? And do you have any money?"

Mik shook his head. He didn't have any money. His two-kroner piece was lying on the little shelf by his bed back home. He hadn't brought it along because he never needed money down by the ruin, and he wanted to save it. But maybe Niels had money; he usually did.

"Anyway, I don't know his number. Do you?" asked Niels.

"No."

"Then how am I supposed to call him up? And what good would it do if we did call?"

"He could send a message . . . and say that we were on our way."

Niels stared down at the highway. "We don't even know where we are," he said.

They stood looking desolately at each other. They had been in situations before, of course, when they might have had a guilty conscience because they were late or had made a promise they couldn't keep, or had done something they had been told not to. And yet this situation was different, because even though the countryside seemed somewhat familiar, they still felt completely foreign here. They simply didn't know what to do. The cars on the highway seemed hostile with their high speed, their self-conscious determination, their closed-in shape. They were lower and more colorful than the cars Mik and Niels had seen before. But they didn't seem any more cheerful for all that. The headlights had disappeared, replaced by glass in front; there was no running board and apparently no turn indicator flag either. The license plates were different too, with more numbers and letters. Most frightening, though, were the huge trucks that rumbled over the concrete with their trailers and poured thick smoke out across the highway. It seemed like an impossible plan to try and stop the cars. How would they go about it?

"We just got lost, that's all," said Niels. He looked defiant.

"What do you mean?"

"We just went around a corner, and we wound up here."

"What about the cave?"

"Oh. There wasn't any cave. All that cave crap!" He shook his head angrily. "That's just you and your stupid imagination. 'Seven holes in your head and a cup of blood.' You really think you're something."

Mik was well aware that Niels was trying to buck himself up by bawling him out. Still he felt a lump in his throat. That's the way it always was when he was scolded. He felt like crying because he thought it was so unfair. And it really was unfair this time. He was just about to retaliate and ask Niels whether he hadn't gone through the cave himself, whether he hadn't seen everything and heard the sounds — and now they knew where they came from — but then he felt somebody approaching. They both turned around at once and saw a tall man come striding across the field toward them. He started shouting and gesticulating even at a distance. But they could understand what he was saying! So they weren't in China after all.

"What the hell are you doing here?" shouted the man. "You don't have any business being here. This is a protected area — and it's private too." He stopped, puffing, and stared at the boys.

"What's the matter, can't you hear what I'm saying?" he panted.

Mik nodded.

"Well then, let's see you get going in a hurry. Or else you'll have me to deal with."

The man kept staring at them. "What are you doing here?"

Niels shifted his feet.

"Nothing," he whispered.

Both he and Mik were used to enraged men chasing them away from places they weren't supposed to be. But it was seldom that the men wore such fine clothes as this strange gentleman. It was also seldom that they were this angry. Most of the time it seemed they were just pretending. But this man was red in the face, almost purple, even though he wasn't very fat. The man opened his mouth again.

"Are you from the Center up there too? You look like you could be, in those getups."

Neither Mik nor Niels knew how to reply, because they had no idea what a center was.

"No," said Mik, trying to think of an explanation. He wanted to say straight out that they had gotten lost and just wanted to go home. But the man seemed so upset, and they couldn't tell him that they had come through a tunnel in the ground and had popped out through a hole in a burial mound that radiated colors — when there weren't even any holes there! Then he'd just get madder.

The man poked the ground with his stick. "I have been up there to complain in person. But of course there's nothing to be done. That sort of person doesn't understand plain Danish. But I don't want any juvenile delinquents and little dope fiends running around my property. You can go tell them that, up there."

He threatened them with his stick. "And we even agreed on it at the property owners' association. We were in total agreement. And it didn't help one bit. They *had* to build that center way out here. In the open air and the healthy country-side, how do you like that, so they could get back on the right foot, the little demons, and run around trampling down my fields. Now will you just get the hell out of here!"

The man swung the stick over his head, and when Mik saw the expression on his face and the purple color spreading around his mouth, he started walking at once. Niels followed close behind, but they could still hear his voice, even though they were getting close to the highway.

"I'm not going to pay taxes and have to sit still while communists and dope addicts wreck my property. I've had enough, and I'm going to put a stop to this outrage, so help me God. What a couple of hippie punks."

Finally the voice faded and was drowned out by the automobile engines and the sound of tires on the concrete. Niels and Mik were now quite close to the road. They could feel the cars rushing by in great shudders, completely taking their breath away. Whenever a truck roared by it made their bodies shake. They crept down into the ditch and sat there huddled together. Mik felt like closing his eyes and holding his hands over his ears and not saying a word, for now he really could tell that they were in big trouble. What was it the man had shouted, and why was he so excited? It was one thing to be thrown out of a strange man's field, but the words he used.

Mik turned to Niels, who had pulled up the collar of his windbreaker around his neck. "What was that he said?"

Niels folded his hands on top of his head. "He was crazy."

"Yeah, but what was it he called us? They were such funny words. 'Dope' — didn't he say 'dope'? Do you know what 'dope' is?"

"No."

"And what else was there?"

"I don't remember."

"That's weird. I didn't understand it. I didn't understand what he said."

"But he sure was crazy."

"Yep."

A feeling of helplessness crept over Mik. He missed his mother and thought about his bed at home in the summer house, where it was very still at night, and the cross of the window frame was outlined in the moonlight on the floor, and the grasshoppers sang outside. And what if they never found their way home?

A sound made him look up. At first he couldn't tell where it was coming from, but then he caught sight of a huge iron-gray insect that came flying low across the concrete road from the east. He poked Niels and pointed. They both got up almost simultaneously. The sound of the aircraft rapidly grew louder, and when it was right overhead it hovered motionless in the air, and a rhythmic flapping sent wave after wave of air down toward them. Niels' hair flew in every direction, and

Mik pulled his windbreaker tight so it wouldn't flap around. Gravel and pebbles flew up from the side of the road and struck their bare legs.

Mik heard Niels shout: "It's an autogyro . . . an autogyro!"

As they stood with the wind whirling around them, feeling as though they would fly off to the left or right any second, the machine rocked slightly back and forth. Without being able to see who it was, they heard a voice descend from a loudspeaker.

"This is the police, this is the police. Get off the freeway, repeat, get off the freeway!"

The aircraft climbed a little, as though it wanted to get a better look. Then the voice came again.

"You down there. This is the police helicopter. Get off the freeway, repeat, get off the freeway. It is highly dangerous and prohibited for pedestrians to be on the freeway."

Niels tried to hold his hair down as he stared at Mik, and it looked as if he were trying to move from the spot where the wind from the aircraft's big propeller held him fast. He looked like he was dancing in jelly, or his legs were glued to the spot. Mik remembered dreams where he had been in the same predicament. He had wanted to run, but couldn't. His legs turned to lead, he couldn't lift them, and the pursuers got closer and closer. For a moment he felt happy because he was convinced that the whole thing was only a dream, but then he saw the autogyro climb even higher and noticed that he could move his feet, and it was real enough. Niels ran a little ahead of him, but when they wanted to go higher up the field, they saw that the angry man was still there. Now they didn't know how close they could stay to the freeway without the helicopter coming back, and it was impossible to go back to the burial mounds and the angry man. Even though they hadn't made a careful search for the hole into the cave, they never would find it now. They just didn't dare go up there.

A hundred yards across the big concrete highway, which the voice had called the "freeway," the helicopter disappeared to the west. The cars passed by as they had done the whole time. It was a long ribbon that never stopped. When they couldn't see the angry man anymore, Mik and Niels headed farther up the field, and when they had run and limped for a while and panted a lot, they came to a lane of dirt and crushed gravel leading off perpendicular to the concrete highway. It seemed quite familiar. They tried to catch their breath. Mik wiped his forehead with his sleeve.

"They must have eaten a long time ago," he said.

It was strange how much that meant. He hadn't thought about it before, but the new situation made the promise to be home for lunch and the meal itself seem larger than life. He had promised his mother that he would come home. He couldn't. He was hungry, but there wasn't anything to eat. At home he would get food, but now he stood here in a strange place and — maybe — in a foreign country and had no money, so he couldn't get anything to eat. Niels was his only hope now.

"Do you have any money?"

"What do you mean, money?"

It was the same old story: Niels always had money, because he never spent any. But he would never admit it, not even now.

"In your coin purse. You usually have a fiver at least."

Time after time Mik had watched Niels take out his boy scout coin purse with the horseshoe clasp and look into it to make sure the money was still there.

"We're going to have to do something!" Mik's voice almost cracked. "I'm hungry."

Niels' expression changed. He stood for a while with his shoulders drooping. "I am too," he said sullenly.

A little later he fished out his coin purse and slowly opened it up. He opened the front flap and looked inside. Then he tried the coin compartment and looked into that. Then he shook his head.

Mik went over to him. "Isn't there any money in it?"

Niels held the coin purse away from him. "Of course there's money in it."

"Well, then what's the matter?" shouted Mik.

"I just have to see how much," said Niels, turning his back.

Mik stood looking at his back and felt like going over and kicking him in the butt. He often felt like doing that, but he didn't dare because he was afraid of losing his friend, and that would never do now that they were completely alone and couldn't find their way home.

"There's twelve kroner," said Niels.

Mik immediately forgot that he wanted to give him a kick. His face brightened with joy. "Twelve kroner!"

Then they would be able to telephone Larsen and take a train home too, no matter where they had wound up.

In Mik's mind twelve kroner was a fortune; he had never had so much money at one time.

"We'll have to find a place to call from."

"I thought you were hungry." Niels looked at him inquisitively.

"Yeah, I am, but it's more important that they find out where we are. You said yourself that they'd go nuts if you didn't show up."

"It's only a loan," said Niels.

"What?"

"If you want something from me . . . some of my money."

Again Mik felt the rage, but he also understood that in order to have twelve kroner in your coin purse you had to be just like Niels. Not only did he have money, he hid it, so nobody knew anything about it — but in this case that was lucky. Mik's stomach growled. There wasn't so much as one flake of oatmeal left in it.

They started walking up the dirt road, and after they had walked for a while they caught sight of a group of buildings that was probably a small town. The houses on the outskirts were quite low and looked pretty much the same; they were rectangular and had black roofs of some sort of roofing felt, or some material that Mik had never seen before. On top of most of them were complicated radio antennas — some in the shape of a cross, others with poles and teeth like a comb. Beyond them were more normal-looking buildings, white-washed, some with tile roofs. They were also equipped with antennas like the ones on the low buildings. Outside several of the houses were automobiles, and as they went by, Mik and Niels looked at the names on them and peeked inside. There were very few they recognized, but "Ford" was written on one of them, and they also found a Fiat, which cheered them up a little, as if they were already home. Even though the cars looked so much different from the few they were used to seeing, they were cars after all, with seats and steering wheels and doors, and some of them had names they had seen before. If they added up their experiences, things weren't all that bad. The angry man in the field had spoken their own language, and the autogyro had too, and now there were the cars that had familiar names, even though there were quite a few they didn't recognize. They felt hungry and confused and a little scared, but they weren't dead — they were still alive.

Mik felt that he had never thought of things like this before, not even when he went through his first air-raid alarm. It didn't occur to him that anything really bad could happen, for his father and mother and sister were sitting next to him in the cellar. Of course he was afraid, but he didn't think — the way he did now — that he was alive and not dead, that you could be alive one minute and dead the next. Now he was convinced that that's the way it was.

They had come to an asphalt road, and after they turned a corner they were standing on what had to be the town's main street. Earlier they had seen a sign with the name of the town in black on a white background with a kind of silhouette below it that looked like houses and towers. From the edge of the curb they looked both right and left. A car drove by; its engine was a little louder than the cars out on the big concrete highway, but it didn't go chug-chug the way they were used to. Niels wanted to cut across the street, but when he stepped out onto the asphalt they heard a loud rattling noise and saw a bicycle coming at them at high speed. The man sitting on it wasn't moving his legs up and down, so it must have been some kind of motorcycle. It was unbelievable that a motor you could barely see could make such a racket. The rider didn't look very old. It was a boy, but it was hard to be quite sure, because he had on a strange, globe-shaped helmet with a transparent glass shield dropped down over his whole face. He sat upright, looking straight ahead, and when he passed by Niels and Mik the noise was so deafening that Mik couldn't help putting his hands over his ears.

They crossed carefully to the other side, as the echoes of the noise still vibrated between the buildings, and the motorized bicycle vanished chattering around a corner. Mik remembered the noise in the tunnel; maybe there was some of it here, but he wasn't sure. Then he thought of the airplanes and the helicopter and the big trucks and the man who had yelled at them. It was a lot of noise at one time — and whenever they thought it was over, it started again with no warning.

Niels had caught sight of a bakery sign. They hurried over to the storefront window. It was full of cakes and French bread, and they leaned forward and stared inside. They hadn't seen so much pastry and so many cream puffs in a long time. For a moment they totally forgot where they were, but then Mik discovered a price tag stuck into a tray of Spandauers. He elbowed Niels and pointed at the sign: "2.50 kr." Niels pointed at another sign on top of the French bread: "4.25," it said. They stared at each other.

"It must be . . . for *all* of them," said Niels.

Mik nodded. There were probably ten or fifteen Spandauers there. They usually cost ten øre apiece, so that meant ten for one krone. Prices must have gone up. Or else they really were in another country.

"What should we get?" asked Mik. He was the one who had to ask. It was Niels who had the money.

"Pastry's no good," said Niels.

Mik felt a pang of disappointment. The pastry looked so delicious. He knew that both his mother and Niels' mother said that there wasn't any nutrition in it. And they had to have nutrition if they were going to withstand this ordeal. He was glad that Niels hadn't yelled at him more about getting lost. Maybe that would come later.

"What about a . . . loaf of French bread?"

Ordinary rye bread was just too boring, since they were having an adventure.

"How are we going to cut it?"

"I've got my knife."

"But then we'll have to have butter too."

"Well, even if it's gone up, can't we afford it anyway?"

Mik could hear his humble voice. He was in Niels' pocket. He wouldn't get any food or find his way home either if he didn't stick with him and behave properly. For a moment he almost regretted having let him in on his secret. But you couldn't get along without a traveling companion and a friend, no matter what he was like.

"We'd better go inside."

Mik didn't like going into stores, but it didn't bother Niels. He took hold of the handle and opened the door. It smelled sweet and delicious in the bakery, and the heat seemed to be on too, although it was summer. At any rate, the air was quite stuffy and still. Mik felt a little dizzy and gasped for air; it was no doubt only because he was hungry.

The bakery lady came in and stood behind the counter, where boxes of candy and chocolate were stacked up too. A couple of the brands had familiar names, but there were a lot of complicated ones and many more than Mik had ever seen before. And chewing gum! He remembered how delicious it was back when they could still get it. Of course his mother didn't like him to chew gum, and she absolutely forbade him to chew bubble gum. But just think if they had enough money left for a pack of gum! He glanced over at Niels, who had his boy scout coin purse out. Music was coming out of the back room. It sounded like a factory, or Wurlitzer music in a movie theater played on a guitar.

"What would you like?" asked the lady.

"A loaf of French bread," said Niels.

The lady went over and got one and banged it down on the counter and wrapped a piece of paper around it and fastened it with a little piece of transparent sticky paper.

"Will there be anything else?"

"Half a pound of butter."

She got it out from a kind of counter that also had margarine and trays of eggs and some white cartons that you couldn't see inside of.

"Anything else?"

Mik poked Niels. "A pack of gum," he whispered.

Niels gave him a dirty look; maybe he hadn't even noticed that there was chewing gum there, or maybe he thought Mik was going too far. But now the word had been said.

"And a pack of gum." He looked at Mik again, a little annoyed, after he had said it.

The bakery lady laid the little package on the counter and went over to the cash register. It didn't look like a regular cash register, and when she pushed the buttons it made funny beeps like little toy car horns.

"That'll be 11.75," she said.

It was quiet in the shop. You could hear the sound of a refrigerator and what must have been the humming of the cash register. It was probably electric. Mik looked at Niels. He was standing stiff, frozen, with his boy scout coin purse in his hand, staring at the bakery lady. 11.75 — that couldn't possibly be right! If they had to pay 11.75 for a loaf of French bread and half a pound of butter and a pack of gum, they would have exactly 25 øre of Niels' money left. And then how would they get home?

Mik got a lump in his throat. He was more at fault than Niels. He was the one who made the frivolous suggestion. If he could only get the bakery lady to take back the gum. He hated the thought, but there really wasn't any choice. He would have to go into action.

"If you could ..."

His voice broke.

"If you could ... couldn't you just ... we don't have much money. If you could just take back the gum."

The bakery lady stared at him malevolently.

"I've already rung it up," she yapped.

The music from the back room changed to a kind of choppy, mechanical rhythm that made the glass counter vibrate and the licorice lozenges quiver. All at once the door opened, and a young man in black leather boots, black leather jacket, and a long garish scarf came in. He had the same kind of helmet on that Mik and Niels had seen when the boy on the bicycle with the motor rode by.

The bakery lady swept the little pack of gum into her hand and threw it back in the box with the other packs of gum.

"10.25," she said.

Niels opened his coin purse and dug his fingers into it and pulled out the two five-kroner bills and the two-kroner piece. He stood a moment with them in his hand, and it looked like he was just about to start crying; then he laid them on the counter top next to the butter and the loaf of French bread wrapped in paper. Mik took a deep breath. He didn't understand a thing; he just felt that something was very very wrong. Two days ago he had bought pastry slices down at Larsen's. He had bought two pieces and knew it was too much, but he wanted them so badly that he couldn't help sacrificing that ten-øre coin.

"What's this?" said the lady.

The boys jumped because it had been quiet so long.

The bakery lady picked up one of the five-kroner bills.

"What do you think this is, Halloween?"

She turned to face the man in the black leather clothes and boots. "I guess they think they can walk in here and pull a fast one."

She stared at Niels and Mik. "What's the big idea, anyway?"

Neither of them knew what to reply, so they just stood there.

"Oh, it's probably a couple of those kids from up at the Home," said the leather man. "They're all crazy as shit. You can see for yourself, the way they look."

The bakery lady put her hands on her hips and leaned forward. Mik could spell out the words on her brown smock: *Los Angeles Fire Department.* Maybe she was from Los Angeles.

"Do you have any money or don't you?"

Niels emitted an unintelligible gurgle. He was blushing all the way up to his hairline, but there wasn't much life in his snaky curls.

"Because I'm damn sure I'm too old to play Monopoly."

She shoved Niels' money over to him and pulled the French bread out of the paper at the same time. "And what the hell kind of getup have you got on? They've got to be punkers. Look at the little one there, those suspenders."

Mik could sense that she was talking about him. He thought he was too old for Tyrolean suspenders too. But people didn't usually talk about them like that.

Niels stuffed the five-kroner bills and the big yellow coin into his coin purse.

"The only thing they need is a good kick in the ass," said the man in black. "If somebody would just give them a good kick in the ass they could save all that medicine and all the people that run around up there farting around. That's for damn sure."

The bakery lady had put the butter back in the glowing counter with all the cartons.

"There are so many weirdos running around these days. You almost don't dare go out on the street at night anymore."

"If we see any of them out at night, we give 'em one on the noodle right away, that's for damn sure. They should at least have to obey the curfew. It's bad enough having to look at them in the daytime."

He turned toward the counter.

"Gimme a pack of Prince and *Ekstra Bladet* and three Elephants, will you?"

"You got bottles with you?"

"Like hell I do. I'll come back in half an hour with the bottles."

The bakery lady looked annoyed, but she went out in back and returned with three beer bottles.

"You can get the paper yourself from the rack."

Mik followed the movements of the man in black and caught a glimpse of a headline on the paper, which looked different than usual: "Millionaire's Sex Life Revealed After Death."

He didn't know what that meant, but there was a big picture on the front page, and the type was so big that it filled almost the whole rest of the page. Mik was still waiting for the man to get the three elephants he had asked for. Maybe it was candy. He scarcely had time to finish his thought when he heard the bakery lady hiss: "Didn't I tell you to get your asses out of here?"

He nodded. They were the only ones she could be talking to.

"Or else I'll help you the hell out," said the man with the helmet and the leather clothes, taking a step toward them. "What a couple of freeloaders."

Niels stuffed his coin purse into the front pocket of his short pants, and then they were actually out on the street again. Before, they had been mostly hungry. Now they were hungry and depressed too.

4

For fun they used to pinch the heads off wheat stalks and eat the kernels. Now they were sitting in the lee of a wheat field, carefully picking kernel after kernel off the stalks and eating them, even though they were green and didn't taste very good. In a couple of gardens they had seen summer apples, but they were green too, and there were often huge dogs behind the fences, or else somebody was home, so they didn't dare try swiping any.

After their experience in the bakery they had no desire to stay in the town any longer. Of course the man had said he only beat up children at night, but they couldn't tell whether he was telling the truth or not. Up until now they had only met three people who had talked to them, and they had all acted hostile, or at least angry. Maybe they had a reason to be mad, because Niels and Mik were doing things that weren't right, things they weren't supposed to do. Still, it seemed as if the people they had met were somehow already mad in advance.

Mik realized that besides the strange headline in the paper about the millionaire and his life after death or whatever it was, he had seen a date — and a year! He hadn't given it a second thought, because there had been other things happening on their way out of town — things that made his head spin. But he thought about it now. What did it say in the paper? It was simply too incredible.

"Did you see what I saw?" he said to Niels.

"Where?"

"On that paper in the bakery."

"Nope."

"I think I saw a date . . . and the year."

Mik's eyes were wide. Some chaff had gotten stuck between two teeth, but when he remembered his discovery he completely forgot to work at the chaff with his tongue.

"Isn't it . . . the 27th?" asked Niels. "The 27th of July?"

"Yeah, but the year! There was another year on the paper!"

"What year?"

"1988. It said the 27th of July, 1988!"

Niels leaned his head on his hand, spitting out some chaff between his feet. "You're always making up stories," he said.

"But it's true. Don't you think it's weird . . . all that other stuff?"

Niels said nothing. He sat with his legs tucked up, resting his head on his knees. Mik didn't know what he should do. He was sure that it had been a different date than 1941. But could it be 1988? 1988! Then he would be almost *sixty* already!

His insides heaved and tugged, as though his bones and muscles and sinews all wanted to go their separate ways at once. Maybe he was sitting there, getting 45 years older all at once, 47 years! It was a horrifying thought. He stared at Niels again; he hadn't changed at all. He was still sitting with his face hidden; his hair curled and moved a little like the wheat stalks in the wind. He had short pants on and the white ankle socks with the blue border; there was no doubt that he was still a boy.

Mik sighed. They had left the bakery and continued down the street. Several times they stopped and looked into other store windows. It was the same way with all of them: the prices seemed unbelievable. A suit cost over 2,000 kroner, a shirt 200 or 150, shoes between 400 and 600 kroner, and when they walked past something they guessed had to be a gas station, they saw on one of the pumps (it looked like a slot machine in Tivoli) that the price of a liter of gasoline was over five kroner!

Still, that wasn't what made the biggest impression on them. In a kiosk they had seen pictures that Mik hardly dared think about. Sure, there were some bits of paper here and there covering the worst spots, but there was no doubt about what the pictures displayed. They were in color and quite graphic; in one place, where the paper had slid up a little, Mik could see that the picture showed a woman with her bottom in the air so you could see everything, and there was another woman in black clothes bending over her with a whip in her hand. There were trickles of blood running down the buttocks of the kneeling woman.

What it meant or what she had done, Mik had no idea.

He only felt a strange, restless heat when he thought about that picture and the other ones; the only thing he could really connect them with was the image of the Phantom and the way he was dressed in the Popeye comic books.

The sound of the wind in the wheat field next to them was soothing. Maybe they could sleep in the field among the stalks if they didn't figure out anything else before it got dark. Naturally he had never slept outside at night before — his mother wouldn't let him — but when he thought about the people they had met, it didn't seem likely anyone would offer to invite them home or to help them at all.

Mik also thought about everything that had been said about "the Home" and "the Center" or whatever it was. Maybe (he didn't dare think the thought through to the end) maybe he and Niels were both crazy, maybe they went crazy all of a sudden and belonged in an institution. Maybe everything they had experienced was only something they were imagining in their madness, and in a little while they would have to go back to their cells, when the prison guards found them, or else maybe the man in the black leather clothes and the boots would come with his friends and give them a "kick in the ass" or "one on the noodle"; wasn't that what he had said?

He lost his nerve again, and he felt a terrible pressure in his throat, just above his breastbone. It wouldn't do any good to cry; they would have to figure something out or they would never get home, and it was already impossible to imagine what their parents were doing now. Maybe they had already called the police; maybe there was a news bulletin about them on the radio. Mik sat bolt upright.

"Maybe we'll be on the news on the radio!"

Niels didn't move.

"Maybe they'll send out an APB."

"And then what?"

"Then we can turn ourselves in . . . at the station."

Niels raised his head. "What if you're right after all?" His voice was hollow. "What if it really *is* 1988?"

A terrible shaking seized Mik. He repressed it with all his might.

"What if it's only this place," he said quickly, stumbling, "what if it's only this place, I mean, we came out somewhere else, it just looks different, but it's the same . . ."

He didn't know how to go on. He thought of his father and mother. He tried to think how old they would be if forty-seven years had really passed, whether they were even still . . .

The idea was too absurd, and he didn't want to take it any further.

"Why don't we try and phone. We've got to call!"

"The money's no good."

"But . . . then can't we borrow a telephone? We can just walk up somewhere and knock on the door and ask if we can use the phone."

"And what if it's far away? We have no idea where we are. And it costs a lot of money." Niels looked at him helplessly. "Everything costs a lot of money. You could see for yourself."

Mik sat for a while, then he said: "If they're listening to the news on the radio, we can sit outside and listen. People turn up their radio loud in the summer all the time, if they're sitting out on the terrace."

He got excited. "And everybody has radios. You saw the antennas."

"How do you know they're radios?"

Mik threw up his hands. "You saw the loop antennas, didn't you? The kind you can buy and put on top of the radio . . ." he lowered his voice " . . . if you want to get the BBC. My dad says you can build one yourself, and maybe we'll get one. Anyway, that's how antennas look, sort of, so they *have* to have radios."

Mik sat for a moment. Then he suddenly got another idea. He shouted right out loud: "Maybe you can exchange the money! Maybe it's just like in a foreign country, where you exchange the money and get new money that's good."

Of course he had never been out traveling, but he did know that that's what you did before the war when you wanted to go abroad. He even felt rather relieved, because that was partly what he had dreamt about so much, both before he had found the cave and even more after he had found it: to go somewhere else, to travel, to see something different, see things change. So there was no point in giving up. His dream had become reality, so he couldn't complain, even though it was really a strange place where they had wound up. Mik stood up.

"Come on," he said, "we're going back to town. Maybe the banks are still open. And if we get the money changed, we'll have time to buy something to eat instead of these stupid wheat kernels."

In disgust he spit out the last hard little bit of chaff and looked at Niels, who was still sitting on the ground.

"What if the guy in black shows up?"

"Well, so what? We haven't done anything, and we can always run."

"And what if he has his friends along?"

Mik let his arms drop.

"We can't stay here until the end of the world."

He wasn't used to seeing Niels so down in the dumps. Usually he was the one who took the lead when something was up, and Mik the one who held back.

"If you never try anything, nothing will ever happen!"

"Uh-huh, and now look what's happened. I'm not only going to get slapped by Anna, I'll get a whipping from my dad. It's all your fault."

Mik got really mad now.

"You didn't have to come along, you know," he yelled. "Nobody forced you to, did they? At first you didn't even believe that there was anything, that the cave even existed, and then you were the one who said we should go through the hole."

He stopped yelling.

"And if you don't get home, at least you won't get a whipping."

Mik said it in a normal voice and could hear that it wasn't quite logical. But he wanted to try to tell Niels that it was better to get home and get a whipping than not to get home at all. It seemed that he understood it too. At any rate he stood up, and after a while they started walking back to town.

It wasn't hard to find a bank, because there were three or four of them, even though the town wasn't very big. They went into one whose name they both recognized. Outside,

Niels handed Mik the coin purse with the money. Maybe Mik would have better luck.

It was very quiet inside the bank — or else they just didn't hear anything, because right when they walked in they both caught sight of the calendar hanging on the wall. There was no doubt about it. There it stood, in black and white: 1988, and below that 27 and then July. The teller gave them a kindly look, and when they had gotten over the shock they went over to him and saw that he was sitting sticking papers into a slot in a machine that emitted a series of sounds which reminded them of the ones the cash register in the bakery made. It ticked and beeped, and then the paper shot out and had both letters and numbers written on it.

"Yes?" said the man.

Mik opened up the boy scout coin purse and took out the two five-kroner bills. He stood a moment with them in his hand, then he laid them on the counter in front of the man.

"Can you change these?" he asked in a low voice.

The teller reached out and pulled the bills over to him. Then he picked them up and looked at them more closely. A moment later he laid them down on the counter and spread them out carefully. Niels squirmed impatiently, and Mik felt that he was blushing a little.

"Where did you get these?" asked the man. He didn't look angry, just curious.

Mik glanced over at Niels. He didn't want to say anything that would get his friend in trouble. But it wasn't Mik's money, after all.

Niels stammered, "From my father."

The man nodded. Then he got up and walked out of the

little enclosure with the bills in his hand, over to another man standing in the background. He showed him the bills, and they talked about them so that Niels and Mik couldn't hear what they were saying. After a while the teller came back. He put the bills on the counter in the opening between the glass partitions.

"These are from before the currency changeover in '45," he said. "Unfortunately I can't give you anything for them."

"'45?" said Mik.

"Yes, in 1945 all the money in the country was exchanged for new. That was to stamp out the hoarding of money. After the war," said the man, by way of explanation.

It was still hard to understand. Mik stared at him, his throat constricting. Then he said, "Yes, but . . . it's Danish money, isn't it?"

"Yes, of course," said the man, "you can see that. It says 'The National Bank of Denmark' and 'Five Kroner.' They just aren't any good anymore, so it must have been some your father had lying around and gave you for fun. But in those days they were worth a lot more than they are now, I can tell you that."

Every time the man said something, it got more complicated. How could five kroner be worth more or less? Five kroner was five kroner!

Mik got another idea. He reached down in the coin purse and fished out the two-kroner coin.

"What about this? Will you change this?"

The man picked up the big yellow brass coin. He held it between two fingers. Then he turned it over and showed that side to the other man.

"2 kr. coin minted 1928. It's legal tender, isn't it?"

The other man came closer. He stopped behind the teller and looked at the coin. Then he nodded.

"Yes, we'll take that."

He looked at the boys.

"But it wouldn't be worth your while. You can get a lot more for it in the city. At least 25 kroner."

"But . . ." Mik's head started spinning again. Five kroner were worth nothing, but for a two-kroner coin you could get at least 25! It was impossible to comprehend.

"I'd be happy to give you a ten for it," said the teller, smiling. It looked as though he were about to pull out his coin purse. But that was apparently too much for Niels. He ran over to the counter where the man had put the two-kroner coin and the two five-kroner bills, scooped them into his hand, and started to run out of the bank.

"I wonder what's gotten into him?" Mik heard the other bank man say; then he ran out himself. Before the door closed behind him, he heard the teller's voice too.

"Oh, they're probably just a couple of those crazy punks from up at the institution."

Out on the street Mik saw Niels, with hunched shoulders, head off in the same direction they had come from. He wanted to shout after him, but now there were more people on the street. It was evidently shopping time, and women were walking along pulling shopping bags on wheels. Some of them had baby carriages too, but the strangest thing was that they all had slacks on. Mik's big sister also wore slacks, but only once in a while. In this town they were everywhere, and when he looked at them more closely he could see that they weren't regular ladies' slacks, but more like some sort of work pants, made of rough blue cloth. A lot of the kids were wearing them too, and when a couple of the noisy bikes with motors on them came down the street, Mik saw that the riders had on the blue pants too. It almost seemed like a uniform, but the scene was still varied because people were wearing everything imaginable with the pants: colored T-shirts with short sleeves or blouses and long scarves, and the helmets the people on the bikes were wearing were painted in glaring colors so bright it almost hurt his eyes.

That was also one reason that everything seemed to swim before his eyes. Everywhere he saw those piercing colors. Spinach-green that didn't look like spinach, red colors that weren't red, and the boxes and buckets at the hardware store weren't made of metal, but of some peculiar material that looked both hard and soft at the same time and was painted in colors Mik had never seen before. They seemed artificial to him, and when he saw a yellow, or almost orange-colored, box with a label on it that said "Lunchbox," he couldn't help thinking of his own. It was made of tin and painted red all over, so it almost looked enameled, and on the lid was written in beautiful letters: "Come and get it."

Mik saw Niels cross the street. It looked as if something had caught his eye. Mik was still thinking about the bank. There were some things his mind just couldn't accept. First the year and then the money. It was not only baffling that the calendar said 1988, it was also unbelievable that the cashier could talk about 1945 and say that the war was over. Was the war really over, and could it have happened without Mik having any clue at all? Was that the way time passed, so that you didn't notice anything at all? He looked down at himself. He could see his sandals and ankle socks and his knees that were brown from the sun. He touched his short pants and then stuck his thumbs in behind his suspenders, as he was in the habit of doing, and stretched them out a little. Everything was the same as when he got up this morning. He suddenly thought about his bike. It was different from the ones he saw here — everything was different — and the only motor he had ever had on it was a clothespin with a string and a piece of cardboard.

He was worried. When his parents started looking for him — and they had certainly started already — they would also search for him at the ruin and the gravel quarry. Maybe at the gravel quarry first, because he and Niels had been told time after time that they were not allowed to play there, and especially not to go near the water or sail out on it. When they found the bikes, would they believe that the boys had gone down to the quarry with the gray water and fallen in? Mik's heart constricted. He could see their faces. He could see his mother crying and his father getting white in the face. He could see his sister . . . and Niels' mother and Anna too. How were they going to take it?

There was no doubt about it: they had to get in touch with their parents, there was no alternative. Mik looked around for Niels and saw him standing with his back to him looking in a store window on the other side of the street. Mik hurried over to him.

What Niels was looking at was a radio store — or at least it looked like a radio store. But there weren't many radios around (if they were radios); on the other hand, the window was full of square boxes with a pane of gray glass in them. The boxes had knobs along the side, and above them were signs with various things written on them: 26″ Color TV, Instant On, or Solid State Remote ZX-2000 Console Cable-Ready Receiver.

As they stood there, one of the panes of glass lit up, and a thin whining tone followed the picture. It didn't show anything, it was just checks and lines in different colors. But right in the middle it said "Radio Denmark."

"What's that?" asked Mik.

"Television," said Niels. He sounded quite decisive and incontrovertible.

"What's that?"

"You can see pictures — through the air."

"Oh, come off it."

The pictures jiggled up and down slightly, and all the sets were whining.

"Don't you remember, just before the war? There were some experiments."

Mik had read something about it, and they had probably talked about "television" too, but if Niels was saying that it was television in the window of the radio store then he must believe . . . then he *did* believe time had passed, that it wasn't the 27th of July 1941, but the 27th of July 1988. Forty-seven years!

He refused to believe it; it couldn't, it mustn't be true. Had so many years really passed — in five minutes? Then almost nobody would be left alive! People forty-five or fifty would be old, really old. They would be almost decrepit and could easily be grandparents or . . . dead. But if he looked down at himself, there was no change, and it was impossible to understand, his mind just couldn't accept it. Maybe they ought to go straight to the police instead of waiting for the bulletin on the radio. Or on television? Maybe that kind of stuff was on television now. There was no way of knowing. If they just waited here, maybe the message would come on right in front of their noses. But how would that work? Their parents didn't know that television had been invented. They had radios and telephones, but television... The pictures flickered inside Mik's head just like the ones on the screens in front of him. It wouldn't do any good to go to the police, not right away at least, because then they'd just get sent up to the Home or the Institution or whatever it was, along with the other "shitheads." No, they needed more time, they had to think it over and figure out a plan. There was also the question of the money. If they could really get 25 kroner for their *daler* in the city — which must mean Copenhagen — then they would have to go there. He tugged at Niels' sleeve.

"Come on," he said, "we have to talk."

Niels nodded absentmindedly.

"I'm hungry," he said.

Mik noticed how hungry he was himself. For a while he had forgotten about it, but now that Niels mentioned it he could feel quite clearly how empty his stomach was. Then he thought of something they used to do back on his street just for fun.

"We can go in and ask for some stale bread," he said. "They always have old bread at a bakery."

Niels shook his head. "Not from her. She's too tough."

"All she can do is throw us out."

"What about the guy in the leather clothes?"

"Shoot, he probably left a long time ago. Come on!"

Mik didn't know where he was getting his courage from. But he had never been this hungry before either. He started sauntering slowly toward the bakery. Niels followed him a little ways behind. The window of the store was still full of bread, but there were more customers inside than before. Mik didn't know whether he should go in at once or wait until there weren't so many people. Then he saw that it was mostly women, and even though they looked different, several of them looked quite a bit like his mother — or at least they were about the same age. Niels had caught up and was standing by the glass door. Then Mik gave him a signal and opened the door.

The radio was still playing the same kind of music in the back room, and every time the beat thumped the glass counter vibrated. It was warm and stuffy inside, but the bread still smelled good, and they were so hungry they felt sick. It was busy, and Mik was amazed at how anyone could eat so much, even if they were really hungry. Some of the women bought five or six loaves of bread, others carried out big bags of rolls, and there was a brisk business in butter and milk. (It turned out that the cardboard boxes had milk in them).

When they finally got up to the counter, and the bakery lady noticed them, she pretended that she didn't see them. Other customers reached up from behind and put money down and picked up merchandise, but finally there was a lady who said that surely it must be the two boys' turn now. The bakery lady looked at them impatiently.

"So, it's you two clowns again, eh?" she said peevishly. "I thought I told you to get lost. What do you want?"

Mik almost didn't dare say anything, but then he got up his courage. It was their only chance, after all.

"Do you have any . . . stale bread?" he asked.

"Stale bread? No, of course I don't have any stale bread! You've got a lot of nerve! We sell all the bread we have, and it's always fresh!"

This last was directed more to the lady in the store than to Mik and Niels. Then she showed her teeth again.

"And I'm going to complain to the Home if you try coming around here again!"

Niels was already on his way out when Mik felt a friendly hand on his shoulder.

"What is it you want?" asked the lady who had let them have their turn.

Mik moved his head back and forth slightly. Then he said in a low voice, "I just asked if there was any stale bread."

"Are you hungry?"

He nodded. Niels had stopped at the door.

"I don't doubt they get plenty to eat up at the narco farm," said another lady in the store.

"Yeah, on our money," quacked a third.

Mik wanted to run out right away, but the lady's hand was still on his shoulder.

"How much are the raspberry slices?" she asked.

"One twenty-five," said the bakery lady.

"Then give them each one."

The bakery lady turned around with a toss of her shoulder

and slid the spatula under the raspberry slices. "I suppose they have to be wrapped up too," she said sarcastically.

"No, just give them one each. We do have to save our natural resources."

Mik could see that the lady was smiling. The others in the store were shifting impatiently.

The lady reached out for the slices and took one in each hand.

"Here you are," she said.

Mik turned around and saw that she was still smiling. Then he took the raspberry slice and bowed deeply, as he had been taught.

"Thank you very much," he said.

Niels came forward and took his slice. Then he bowed too, and his long hair fell forward so that his snakelike curls wiggled, and he said in his deeper voice, "Thank you very much."

The bakery lady giggled. "What a couple of clowns," she said to the people in the store, "or maybe they're just acting fresh. I wouldn't put it past them. Will there be anything else?"

The last remark was surly, and a voice in the back added, "Yeah, we can't stand around waiting all day."

Out on the street the boys started running, as though they were afraid that what had just happened wasn't true, or that the lady would take back the raspberry slices if they didn't get out of there and disappear fast. They raced in and out among the pedestrians, several of whom turned to stare at them in irritation. Finally they reached the edge of town and found the little dirt road where they had sat before in the lee of the wheat.

Both of them tried to control themselves, but as soon as the mixture of dough and sugar and the sweet raspberry taste had touched the tip of their tongues, it was next to impossible to stop from wolfing down the whole piece of pastry in one gulp. In less than two minutes they were eaten up, and it wasn't until afterwards — as Mik felt a new energy arise in him like a tickle — that he realized that he and Niels had just eaten two raspberry slices, which cost a total of 2½ kroner, and which in reality only cost 10 øre!

He sat for a while and chewed on the phrase "in reality," and suddenly he felt that he didn't really know what it meant.

It was gradually starting to get dark. The sun hung low in the sky; this was the time of day his mother usually told him to put on a sweater. Thank God they had the windbreakers with them, but it would still get cool if they had to sleep out in the wheat field with nothing over them. If only he had been a boy scout, then Mik would have known something about making a fire and setting up camp, but his mother and father didn't want him to join. They thought it was better for him to sleep in his bed at night, not in a tent.

"I'm still hungry," said Niels.

Mik was too. Still he felt as though a little warm rocket had been shot off inside his body. "What do you think that is, anyway?"

"What?"

"What they keep talking about all the time. That home."

"It's probably some kind of reform school."

"So do they ever get to go out?"

Niels shrugged. "It's called something else too."

Mik sat there for a while, then he said: "Maybe we should have gone up there."

Niels turned his head. "Are you crazy? Didn't you hear what they said?"

"What did they say?"

"You know, the way they talked about it. It must be horrible up there."

"Sure, but what if that's where we belong?"

"Oh, come off it. We haven't done anything!"

Mik was silent again. Then he said, "I suppose you could say that we . . . ran away from home."

Niels shook his head, annoyed. "Yeah, but we couldn't help it — not really. It wasn't something we wanted to do, after all."

"We . . . we wanted to go into the cave."

"But we didn't have any idea where it would lead!"

They both fell silent. It was as if the same question was rattling around inside both of them: Where *did* it lead?

"Now I've heard that word twice already — *narco*. What do you think it means?" said Mik after a while.

"It must be something . . . dirty. Something they did."

"It sounds creepy."

Niels looked around. "It's creepy *here*," he said.

The wind moved through the grain, and the sound was soothing and familiar. But this was when the swallows should have been there! You always noticed them at twilight, the way they swooped low over the fields and swung up into the vanishing light to catch the last insects before the bats came out and took over the hunting grounds. But there wasn't a bird in sight; nothing moved, nothing sang. Only the wind rustled through the grain. Mik remembered the sound from the colored screens in the show window of the radio store. It was as though a little of that sound was out here in nature too.

Hopelessness sneaked in between the two of them, and it was some time before either of them said anything. Niels had lain down on his side and pulled up his knees; Mik was still sitting up straight and looking around. They could have talked to the friendly lady in the bakery, that would have been the thing to do. And even the man in the bank was friendly, even though he did say something about the kids at the Home. Or was that his colleague? In any case they would have to talk to somebody, and the language at least was pretty much the same. They had received what they had asked for until now, or had been scolded when people suddenly got annoyed.

Mik tried to figure out what people really had said, and why the language didn't seem quite like the one he was used to hearing and speaking. First of all, there were a lot more angry people — the man in the field, the bakery lady, the guy in the black leather clothes — but maybe it was all just a coincidence, because there had been nice people too. They all just talked louder and used different words than he was used to. Some of them he didn't understand at all — *narco*, *hippie* (was that it?) — and when he thought about the horrible machines that had flown over their heads, he realized that they probably didn't even have propellers on them! How was it possible to fly without propellers?

Mik also thought about the huge purchases being made in the bakery. Maybe people had started having more children — or else they were hoarding. Here was a word he knew! Even though his mother and father said they weren't supposed to hoard things, they had still bought plenty of sugar and flour and tobacco when the occupation came. But the man in the bank had said that the war was over. The whole thing was totally confusing. Anyway, there wasn't anybody using ration stamps in the bakery, and there seemed to be enough food.

Mik noticed that Niels looked smaller and frailer than he usually did, as he lay there at the edge of the wheat field. They would often flop down on the shoulder of the road with their bikes when they didn't feel like riding any longer, or when there was a great view, and it was almost always Niels who decided when; in fact, he usually decided everything. He was the one who went into the tunnel first too, and even when Mik stood there with the very end of the kite string in his hand, Niels kept egging him on, even though he was scared. Now it seemed as though Niels had given up. Or was he just tired?

It was easy to hurt him, Mik knew. They were both sensitive, but here his friend lay, seeming quite vulnerable. He looked defenseless, and it was impossible to guess how the night would pass. There wasn't any shoulder along the road either. Mik hadn't seen a single one in the new landscape. "Back home" there were shoulders along all the roads covered with tall flowers and grass. Here it looked like they were mowed or completely leveled off. So they would have to tramp into the wheat field or find another place to sleep. The best thing to do, of course, would be to go back to the field and the burial mounds and find the hole to the cave. It *had* to be there, and the man couldn't be running around out there at night too! First they had to hear the evening news — or watch it. Were you supposed to *watch* it? And then they had to find their way back.

"What are you thinking about?" he asked softly.

Niels didn't answer right away. Then he said, "We're never going to get home."

"Sure we're going to get home." Mik didn't sound convincing. "We just have to find somebody nice . . ."

Niels sat up and pulled his windbreaker around him. There was gravel stuck to one sleeve.

"This isn't even Denmark," he said, "this isn't even our own country!"

"Sure it's our country. The people speak Danish, don't they?"

"Hmph," said Niels.

"You can understand what they're saying, can't you?"

"Yeah, but it's still like they're sort of not talking to you. And the things they say sound weird."

"That lady was nice."

"Yeah, but she was the only one."

"Maybe there are some others."

Niels brushed off his sleeve. "They think we're crazy. Or criminals."

"But we're not doing anything."

"That's another reason why it's so creepy. We haven't done anything, but they're all mad anyway."

"Well, we *were* in the man's field . . ."

"Sure, but we couldn't help it! We can't help any of it. It's all wrong anyway. Our money, and the way we look, that's what makes them mad. What else could it be?"

Mik pulled his knees up under his chin. "Larsen's is closed now."

"Larsen's! There isn't any Larsen, there hasn't ever been any Larsen. And what good would it do if there was? We don't have any money anyway."

It was an impossible thought that Larsen the grocer didn't exist. Mik didn't have to close his eyes to be able to see his face. He was short and fat with a red face, and he wore Tyrolean hats and suspenders. He always had a cheroot in his mouth. He didn't say much, but he never scolded you either. If Larsen the grocer didn't exist — then their fathers and mothers and Anna and Mik's sister Gudrun and Niels' big brother Ole didn't exist either. Then there wasn't anything in the whole world but what was here, and if that was true it might as well be the end of the world. If they hadn't been there themselves, that is — but they were. He felt quite sure that it was him, Mikkel Paslund, who was sitting there, and his friend Niels Storm sitting across from him. He could reach out his hand and touch him. Just to be sure, he did, and Niels stared at him.

"What is it?"

"Nothing. I just wanted to see if you were there."

Mik couldn't help smiling. It was just too crazy. Of course they were there — with flesh and blood and ankle socks and windbreakers and everything. Even if it was suddenly 1988 or 1990 or 1998, or whatever. The earth was there too, in spite of everything. He could see it, they had been walking on it, and even though it was scary and didn't smell good, and most of the people seemed strangely unsatisfied and angry, the world did exist, and there couldn't be any doubt about that.

"Come on," he said to Niels, "we'll have to go back before it gets dark. We can't sleep out here tonight."

"Why not?"

"It's too cold here."

"Where are we going to go?"

"Didn't you want to call home?"

"I told you that Larsen . . . and the money's no good!"

"I'm sure that they're going to put out a bulletin on us."

"Who?"

"Our parents."

"If they exist . . ."

Mik got up. He was mad.

"You stop saying that," he said.

He was in doubt himself, but he wouldn't stand for his friend talking that way. Now it was time for something to happen!

"Well, *I'm* going, at least," he said.

He turned and strode off toward the town. A little later he could hear that Niels was following.

5

As darkness fell, a peculiar sound spread through the town. As the boys wandered back they could see that men were walking around on the lawns with little machines that made noise and cut the grass. They must be motorized lawnmowers. Almost every house had one, and outside every gate a car was parked. The houses were almost identical, and it was hard to tell the difference between the men cutting the grass. They all had on blue work pants too, and short-sleeved sweaters or shirts. The sound from the lawnmowers made it impossible for Niels and Mik to talk to each other. The men in their yards couldn't talk to each other either; the noise was too loud. Little by little it died out and was replaced by another noise. Through the open patio doors and windows came the sound of music, followed by a voice that said "good evening." The boys pricked up their ears, because it had to be the News of the Air from Radio Denmark. At the same time as the voice started, there was a change in the light coming from all the doors and windows. A bluish, flickering glow fell across the flower beds and lawns. Or else it shone up on the ceiling and cast a ghastly reflection through the windows and doorways. When they looked around, there wasn't a soul to be seen in the front yards anymore. They must have all gone inside.

"Television," whispered Niels, "it's television."

Mik glanced at him and saw that the flickering light made his face look the way it had down in the cave. Shadows danced across his face, all his features ran upward and curved, and his hair was alive again, as if it were full of snakes.

"Come on," he said, "we've got to see this!"

Mik hesitated. Now they were certainly going to do something forbidden again. It was their only chance if they wanted to hear the bulletin about themselves. For a moment they scanned the hedge, then Niels spotted a hole at the bottom, where a dog probably tried to get in and out when the gate was locked. Just as in most of the other houses, a window stood open in the house behind the hedge, and they could still hear the voice talking — interrupted now and then by other loud sounds — and the light was flickering out across the lawn. Right under the window there were bushes in a flower bed; maybe they could hide there and then crawl up to the window and see what was happening and hear what the voice was saying. It didn't make any difference that the broadcast had already started; the bulletins always came at the end.

Niels got down on his knees and crawled in through the opening. The leaves rustled, but the noise wasn't as loud as the sound of the voice. A little later Mik followed him. In the twilight they ran across the strangers' lawn and made it into the darkness among the bushes. They were rhododendrons, Mik noticed, but there weren't any flowers on them; it was too late in the season. In the dark they signaled back and forth, and then Niels crawled up on a little brick molding that went all the way around the house, and Mik pushed him up from behind and held him there so he could reach up over the window frame and look in. It wasn't long before Mik started thinking he was getting pretty heavy. But they hadn't agreed on how long Niels was supposed to stay up there, so Mik exerted himself and could feel how his friend's tailbone bored into his shoulder. At last Niels slid back down, and they stood side by side.

"What was it?" whispered Mik.

"Pictures," said Niels.

"Sure, but what kind of pictures?"

"It was television. The whole family was sitting in front of the set. You could see all kinds of things!"

"Like what?"

"I don't know. I couldn't really tell. It looked so weird, it was all mixed up."

"Was it . . . a bulletin?"

"No." Niels stood in silence and looked totally forlorn.

"There was a lot about war," he said.

Mik was getting annoyed. As if there wasn't always a lot about war. But the man in the bank had said that the war was over many years ago . . .

"Let me try it."

He stretched out his arms to Niels to get a boost up. Soon he got his foot up on the molding and pulled himself up over the edge of the window. What Niels had said was true. A big set with flickering colors stood in the middle of the room, and in front of it sat a man and a woman and three children, staring at the pictures. Their faces looked like Niels' face. They were alive and in motion without changing their expression. Mik tried to see what the pictures were about, but they kept changing, and it was hard to follow what was going on because he didn't understand very many of the words the announcer was saying. He heard "escalation" and "negotiating posture" and "satellite country," but he had no idea what any of it meant, and it got even worse when the announcer started talking about "nuclear weapons concentrations" and "cruise missiles" and "radioactive fallout." The viewers in the living room looked worried, and Mik noticed that the woman moved her hand over to her husband's as they stared at the pictures. It was hard to stand so long in the same position, and he knew how hard Niels was straining underneath him. But he didn't dare climb down, because if a bulletin came on now . . .

The broadcast went on and on, and he watched pictures of huge tanks and big bombs standing in rows and pointing up to the sky, and suddenly formations of the eerie propless planes came zooming across the picture with the same sound they had heard out in the field. Mik's legs started shaking — both because of fatigue and because things were all starting to run together inside his head. There was too much to figure out all at once, and it didn't look like there was going to be a bulletin from his father and mother after all. At that moment he heard a new sound that made his hair stand on end. He could also feel that Niels was starting to get restless underneath him. At first he didn't understand what it was, because the television was making so much noise, but then he recognized the sound. It was the same deep, forbidding growl you heard if you got too close to Jens Ewald's dog. It was a rumbling, whistling wheeze that would soon turn into loud barking and raised hackles and bared teeth if they didn't get out of there fast. The foundation began to shake under Mik, but before he reached the ground the dog had started barking, and before he lost sight of the family in front of the set in the living room he saw that the man got up and stared intently at the window.

In front of the rhododendron bush the dog was blocking their way to the hedge and the hole in it. Behind them was the wall of the house. To the right was the garden gate. The light from the set in the living room was reflected off the ceiling into the dog's eyes, which shone yellow so that Mik thought for a moment that there must be light bulbs inside them. In front of the floppy jowls its canine teeth gleamed like sabres. The boys squeezed together, and Mik backed up against the wall so hard that he could feel the bricks scrape against his head. Neither Müller's nor Jens Ewald's dog had ever been so terrifying as the one standing in front of them now.

Suddenly the door opened, and the man stepped out into the yard. The dog got wilder. It dug its paws into the ground and backed up as it opened its mouth all the way and spewed sound at them. Then they heard the man's voice.

"Rex," he shouted. "What is it, Rex?"

Through the twilight they could feel him coming closer. He walked carefully, searching, as if he expected to discover the worst. At the same time he kept calling the dog. Maybe it had just found a porcupine.

At that very moment Niels started to run. He didn't get three steps before the dog was on top of him. It sank its teeth into the sleeve of his windbreaker, but Niels was going so fast that he made it halfway to the hedge while the dog chewed on the piece of cloth it had torn off. When Mik took off too, and the man kept calling and shouting, the dog got so confused that it didn't know which way to turn. It spun around in a circle twice before the man grabbed hold of its collar. By that time the boys had vanished.

But in the distance they could still hear the man shouting. Above the murmur of voices from the television sets all around they could hear him yelling that if they ever set foot on his property again he wouldn't hold back his dog, and that these peeping toms had to be stopped once and for all, and he wouldn't stand for it anymore, because there had to be a limit to the perversions normal people had to put up with, and everything was going to hell, and it was all their fault . . .

The words flew over the hedge and shot out on both sides of them and only died out when they had gone far down the road and had turned a couple of corners. Only every third streetlight was lit; but when they thought they had gotten far enough away from the house and felt a little safer, Niels stopped in the light to inspect the damage. The rip in his windbreaker was at least eight inches long and the hole over two inches across. Niels let his arms drop.

"Well, we might as well stay here now," he said.

Mik could understand what he meant. There was no point in going home with their clothes in this condition. Still, that wasn't what discouraged him the most. He knew how much clothes meant to Niels, and how hard it was to get any

new ones because of the present circumstances. The problem
was to find out just what kind of circumstances they were
dealing with. He hadn't completely caught his breath yet, and
stood there puffing and listening to his heart, which was
pounding hard. Deep inside he had no idea what was going
on, but one thing was becoming more and more clear: wherever they were, and no matter what they did, they made
people mad. Of course they weren't always where they were
supposed to be, but everybody they met seemed to get more
worked up than necessary. They sneered and snapped at
them, and even yelled and shouted. And that dog! Mik had
never seen anything so terrifying. He got a chill down his
spine just thinking about it.

In order not to attract any attention, they stepped out of
the light a ways and stood in the shadow on the sidewalk.
Inside a jasmine bush that had lost its flowers, a bird moved
restlessly.

"What now?" Niels asked hoarsely.

"We'll have to go to the police."

"And then what?"

"If our parents have told them we're missing, then the
police will know."

"Yeah, but it isn't even the same police. They aren't our
police at all. Nothing is ours!"

"No," Mik said softly.

"And if the man reports us . . . Everybody wants to report
us. Then what?"

Mik smiled a little. "We did get something to eat though."

"What if they beat us up and throw us in jail . . . or sic the
dogs on us?" He shuddered.

After a while Mik said, "If only we could find that lady." He smoothed his hair. "I'm hungry. And it's cold."

A shadow — which they hadn't noticed at all — suddenly slid up beside them. They both jumped. The shadow stopped. It was a person about their size, but dressed in a funny way. A wide-brimmed hat, which looked like it could have belonged to Mik's father, camouflaged the stranger's face completely in its darkness. The sleeves of his jacket were so long that they reached all the way down over his hands. Only the pants looked normal. They were the ordinary blue work pants everybody wore.

"Hi," said the Shadow.

Neither of them answered. There was a pause, then the Shadow said, "Cat got your tongue?"

Niels cleared his throat.

"Well, maybe you could give me a light, then."

Mik was just about to say no, but then he remembered Niels' matches, or his brother Ole's, to be exact.

The Shadow had pulled out a cigarette butt and stuck it in his mouth. Niels rattled his box of matches. Then he handed them to the stranger. The Shadow took the box, then weighed it in his hand. He stepped a little farther into the light and stared at it.

"What the hell is this?" he asked.

Mik didn't know what he meant, but he replied, "Matches."

In the light it was easier to see what the Shadow looked like. Judging by his voice he wasn't much older than Mik and Niels — when you looked at him, it was obvious. Well, maybe he was thirteen. He had cheap welfare glasses on, and that made his face look a little familiar, but it still seemed foreign. His eyes looked older than he did.

"I've never seen anything like this."

He opened the box. "But these are high-class." He struck one and lit the butt.

"Real wood," he said.

He was about to stuff the box in his pocket, but remembered Niels and handed it to him. The darkness obscured the contours of his face, and only the lenses of his glasses gleamed under the wide hat brim when he moved his head.

"Are you out taking a walk too?" he asked.

Again neither of them knew what to answer. Mik mumbled something that sounded like "yes." The Shadow didn't seem angry, but still they had to be careful.

"Once in a while you've got to be yourself, right?"

He stepped closer and stared Mik and Niels in the face.

"But I don't think I recognize you two. Aren't you from the institution? What the hell kind of strangeoids are you? Well, I guess I shouldn't ask so many questions . . ."

He stepped back into the shadows again. Then he remembered something and held the cigarette butt out to Niels.

Niels hung his head. "I don't smoke."

"Who the hell asked if you smoked? Take a hit, it's good shit."

Niels shook his head.

The Shadow looked at Mik.

"How about you? It's a drag to get loaded all by yourself." He looked at the butt. "Even though there isn't much of a load in a roach like this. You got anything better?"

"We're . . . we're strangers," said Mik. "We're . . . not from this town."

"From this town? God, no. I'm not either, thank God in heaven. Then you might as well be dead to start with. But what are you going to do? Not that I'm curious or anything."

He held the glowing butt with both fingers and sucked the smoke deep into his lungs and held it. When he exhaled again, he looked at Mik with a little smile.

"You've got to excuse me, man, but I'm afraid I bogarted it that time." He closed his eyes. "Although that's totally against my principles."

Suddenly he burned himself and threw the hot ash to the ground. He cursed softly, then he threw his arms wide.

"If I'm fast enough I can get in on the sleeping-pill group. Nobody will know I'm gone, they're all sitting staring at the damn tube. Now something's finally happening."

He ground the ashes out with his foot.

"You look a little down in the dumps. Did somebody piss on your jelly sandwich?"

For a moment Mik wondered whether he knew they had eaten some raspberry slices, but then he could see it was impossible. The Shadow's shoes were two colors — gray and blue — and they looked like some kind of gym shoes. Maybe he was a gymnast, but they didn't usually take sleeping pills, especially not kids. Mik had no idea what he should say.

"So if you're not from town, where are you from? Yeah, excuse me for asking, but I can't imagine anybody would come here of their own free will."

Mik hesitated, then he said: "We got lost."

"Lost? I didn't think you could in this country. With all these pigs."

They didn't understand. "Pigs?" said Mik.

The Shadow stared at him. "Yeah, you guys are weird all right. Don't you know what a pig is?"

"No."

"How about a cop then?"

"Uh, sure . . ."

"A pig is a cop, and a cop is a pig. Listen, you guys must be really lost, huh? Where do you live?"

"We're on vacation," said Niels.

There was no way to explain it. How were they supposed to tell him that they came out of a burial mound and now everything was different? Could they tell him about the cave and the sounds and the colors? And how could they say that in reality it was the 27th of July, 1941, when it said everywhere that it was 1988? The boy would think they were crazy for sure, and that would never do. They would have to make up a story.

"We were taking a walk," Mik said vaguely.

"And so you wound up here? Jesus Christ," said the Shadow. He stood there for a moment, then he folded his hands so his long sleeves covered them completely.

"Well, that's sort of like it is with me, I don't belong anywhere either, I'm on sort of a vacation too . . . up in the flippo factory, but not because I want to be. Though it's good to come down a few notches once in a while."

Again, neither of them understood a word. Was there a flipper factory in the town? Did the boy work there? And what was that he was saying about notches? He might as well have been speaking another language.

Niels got up his nerve. Whenever they were down as far as they could get, he was always the one who broke through.

"You . . . you don't have anything we could eat, do you?"

"Eat? I told you I was completely clean."

Niels collapsed again. The Shadow looked at him curiously. "Oh, I get it. You mean *food*, something to eat?"

"Yeah."

The boy slapped his forehead. "Holy shit, food! He thinks I run around with food on me. Nope, I don't have any food. So you're hungry, are you?"

They both nodded.

"For crying out loud."

He moved his head so it shifted between shadow and light, making his glasses glint. Then he took off his hat and scratched his head. His hair stuck straight up, and as far as they could see in the semi-darkness it was carrot-colored. For a moment he reminded them of Mik's old Uncle Valdemar. He had a haircut that made his hair stand straight up from his scalp too. But he was an old man!

"Well," said the strange boy, "if you're hungry we better see about getting you something to eat. That's always a way to kill an evening. I sure don't feel like sitting and looking at all that war shit."

He waved his hand. "This way."

They strolled past the fences until they came to what the boys by now recognized as the main street. Before they got there the Shadow turned around and stopped them.

"There aren't any regular all-nighters in this town, but the cafeteria down by the station is open late. They're usually good for a spring roll and a bag of fries. But what about some cash? I don't even have any change on me."

"We don't either," said Mik. "We have some money . . ."

He regretted instantly that he had blurted out their secret.

Niels finished the sentence: "But it isn't any good."

Now the Shadow stared at them as if they were really crazy. He pushed his hat to the back of his head.

"I've met a lot of crazy jokers," he said, "but you two take the cake. First one of you says you don't have any money, then the other one says you do, but it isn't any good. This sounds like a game show or something. What do you *mean*?"

Niels pulled out his boy scout coin purse and opened it. Suddenly he was acting like a conspirator. He fished out the two-kroner piece. Then he went over to the Shadow.

"This is it here," he said. "It's a two-kroner piece."

"OK, let's see it. Two kroner, huh? There isn't anything called a two-kroner piece."

"See for yourself." Niels handed him the coin.

The boy took it and held it up to his eyes, scrutinizing it. Then he read: "2 kroner. Denmark 1928."

He looked at them.

"Oh, one of those old clunkers. Well, it isn't worth shit."

"Yes it is," said Niels, "and it's worth a lot more than two kroner. We went to the bank with it ourselves, and they said that we could get at least 25 kroner for it . . . in the city."

"In Copenhagen?"

"Yeah."

The Shadow whistled appreciatively through his teeth. "Well," he said, "I know there are some people who go totally bananas over old crap like that." He pulled his hat down on his forehead. "In that case we'd better take good care of it."

Niels carefully put the two-kroner piece back in his coin purse.

"But then you won't get anything to eat, that is, not unless . . ." The Shadow got a sneaky look on his face, and then he made a sign and they followed him down the main street.

It was almost empty; from the apartments above the shops they could hear the sound of the televisions through the open windows. The lights in the display windows were turned off (if they had ever been turned on), and they sensed their own figures as shadows every time they passed one of the black surfaces. Halfway down the street they heard a noise behind them that got louder and louder and finally grew to a thundering roar. Before they had a chance to look around, the Shadow grabbed hold of their sleeves and dragged them into the gap between two buildings. From there they could see that the sound was coming from ten or twelve big motorcycles that zoomed past and vanished in a dark clump with their headlights playing over the pavement.

"The Iron Gang," whispered the Shadow. "Rockers and baby rockers too. Stay away from them unless you want somebody on your ass."

Mik recognized the uniform. The motorcycle riders all had on boots and black leather clothes and helmets with thick celluloid in front.

The noise died away slowly. They couldn't tell if the

motorcycle riders had ridden out of town or whether they had just stopped somewhere up ahead.

"They're probably at the cafeteria," said the Shadow. He got a sly look in his eye. "So we can go to work in the meantime."

They turned a corner and came out on a little square paved with cement, where the post office was, and next to it a store with a "Laundromat" sign outside. In front of the post office there was something they guessed had to be a telephone booth. The Shadow held them back.

"Well, now we have two possibilities," he whispered, "and here we're talking degree of difficulty one and degree of difficulty two. And rewards according to the difficulty."

When they heard the Shadow speak, he definitely seemed older than Mik and Niels, even though he might not be any older at all.

"The phone booth is simple enough, all it takes is a good whack, then it'll spit out two or three kroner; but if we take on the laundromat, then it's more serious. On the other hand, the laundromat is full of fivers. If the old lady hasn't taken them home already, that is."

"You mean you want to *break in*?" Niels' voice was very soft.

"I wouldn't call it breaking in. I just happen to know about a window around back that isn't too hard to get open . . . and we could have forgotten something. Don't you ever leave anything at the laundromat?"

Niels shook his head. Sometimes they sent out washing and ironing, but then a delivery boy brought the clothes in a big basket.

The Shadow made a motion with his hand for them to stay where they were. Then he looked both ways and went over to the phone booth and opened the door. He held it open with one foot. Then he raised his hand and banged it against the side of the telephone. Nothing happened. Mik glanced around at the buildings nearby, but there wasn't a soul to be seen. Only the sound of the various voices from the televisions could be heard as a soft murmuring. The Shadow hit it one more time, still in vain. Then he came back out.

"That's just for amateurs anyway," he sneered. "Chicken feed!"

They pulled back out of the light and studied the "Laundromat" sign. Were they all of a sudden going to be involved in committing a burglary? Just the words themselves sounded so serious and creepy: "committing a burglary." When he was lying in bed this morning, Mik would have sworn that he would never get into a situation where he would have to steal — and especially not to get something to eat. Maybe it was still too early, maybe they shouldn't have given up so soon. After all, there had been *one* person in this town who had treated them kindly and had even given them something to eat. The image of the lady emerged. She could have been their mother, and she was just as kind as Mik's mother would have been if she had suddenly run into two hungry boys in a bakery. Where was she now? Would they ever be able to find her, and would she help them again?

The questions were mounting up. Mik thought too, that in the few hours that had passed, he had made more decisions than in the whole rest of his life almost. And now he was possibly standing before the most serious of them all. If he let the Shadow break into the laundry and steal money, then he was . . . an accomplice. He and Niels would both be accomplices. What would happen if they didn't get any money, if nothing happened at all? At worst they would starve to death. He felt his stomach cramping, he wasn't used to going without food for so many hours, but of course they could survive until tomorrow, they could easily go to sleep without food for once. Maybe then they could get some work tomorrow, work in a field, run errands . . .

He was just about to stop the Shadow, but Niels held him back. "What's the matter?" he whispered.

"This is burglary," Mik said.

"Haven't you ever stolen anything?" Again Niels' face was shining, moving.

"Me?"

"Yeah."

"I don't think so."

Niels stepped closer. "Sure you have. Don't you remember that time in the candy store? and my brother's bullets? and the time we stole 25 øre from Anna, from the plate shelf?"

Mik remembered all that. But that was kid stuff. That was nothing, it wasn't burglary.

The Shadow had returned.

"If you guys don't shut up and stop yelling we're going to have the whole town on our neck in five seconds."

Niels took a deep breath. Mik stared at the strange boy, who suddenly made a sign to him.

"Come on," he said, "I can't get through that window by myself."

A chill ran through Mik, then he cast a glance at Niels' face, which the lone streetlight turned into a mask. He felt alone, he didn't want to do it. He belonged with his own kind, but if he did it he would have to follow the Shadow.

Around in back of the laundry building it was almost pitch dark. The back wall — made of some kind of rough cement with edges and all bumpy — abutted a sloping grass embankment, and as they walked along it Mik caught sight of the opaque window that sat up under the building's flat tar-paper roof. It was about six feet up to it, and if the Shadow was going to get in that way, he would have to get up on Mik's shoulders. It might get to be a habit to have people standing on your shoulders.

They gestured to each other as well as they could in the dark, and before the Shadow crawled up, Mik showed him his knife. The boy nodded eagerly, a reflection glinted off his glasses, and it looked like he was smiling. Then he stuck the knife blade between his teeth and signaled that he was ready to climb up. Mik felt his hands around his neck and his feet pushing off, then he was up, while Mik with all his might braced himself against the grass embankment and tried to keep his balance.

As he stood there — a double man — the thoughts began to well up again. He was scared, although less scared than he would have thought just a minute ago — or that morning or yesterday or the day before. The whole thing seemed too strange for him to really be able to take it seriously or connect it with anything to do with himself. Still he was the one who was standing there in the dark in a strange town with a strange boy on his shoulders in the process of committing a burglary. Though it felt strange and unreal, the hunger was real enough, and since they had apparently lost contact with their parents and the world that had been theirs until a few hours ago, then it probably wasn't so odd that now they were doing things they had never dreamed of doing before. Niels' face hovered before his eyes in the dark. What kind of strange mood swing was it that always happened with him? One minute he was more timid and withdrawn than Mik had ever been, and then suddenly he was making decisions and doing totally surprising things that you never would have expected of him.

The Shadow's heels bored into Mik's shoulders every time he strained, leaned forward, and pried at the window. The soles of the gym shoes were hard, and they emitted an odor that seemed chemical or synthetic, like bakelite. Mik heard the gnawing sound of the knife in the woodwork, then it seemed that the Shadow took a break.

"What is it?" whispered Mik.

"I'm just about there," the Shadow whispered back. "I've almost got hold . . ."

Mik felt his legs move under him. He didn't have much strength left.

"Try . . . try and move back a little. I've got to get my fingers in . . . so I can pry it open."

The Shadow clamped his legs around Mik's head. Mik was just about to yell, but he knew he couldn't, so he slowly moved his feet back while the other boy struggled in the dark.

"Lean forward a little . . . that's it."

He did, but he felt like forgetting the whole thing and letting go and running away. He couldn't stand it, but somewhere deep inside he felt a kind of pride. He was doing the impossible. He could endure something he never would have believed he could.

All at once the window burst open, and the weight shifted surprisingly on his shoulders; but before he could get his balance, they both heard an insane, oscillating wail that seemed to come from inside the laundry. It came so suddenly that at first they didn't think it had anything to do with them, but it still made the Shadow's feet slip on Mik's shoulders, and both of them tumbled back into the darkness toward the grass embankment. For a moment they lay there, then the Shadow gasped: "A burglar alarm . . . the bitch got a burglar alarm hooked up!"

He jumped up at once, and Mik followed as best he could. In a flash he realized that everything that was forbidden to happen had happened, in less than five minutes. A word throbbed in his mind, and after a while it emerged, a word he knew from reading books: "outlaw." Now he was an outlaw!

Around the other side of the building by the post office and the phone booth on the little square stood Niels, with both hands over his ears. He was pressing them hard against his skull and had shut his eyes, as if he could keep out all the scary things that way. The sound coming from the siren or burglar alarm kept on and on, and even as they stood there on the square, not knowing what to do, people started appearing in the windows, and lights were turned on all over the place.

The thing that made them start running was the sound of motorcycles getting closer and closer, blending with the noise from the siren. For a moment Mik felt as though the two different sounds were boring in from both sides and meeting in the middle, threatening to blow up his skull. He got his feet moving and saw that Niels was running too, but out on the main street they already ran into the light from the motorcycles sweeping across the pavement; there seemed to be no way to escape. The machines got closer and closer, and when they rode up onto the sidewalk too, Mik saw that the silhouettes behind the blinding headlights were all the same kind he had seen in the bakery: black leather jackets, aviator glasses, and helmets with face shields. He heard a voice call above the noise of the engines: "It's them . . . it's them again!"

Then a big front wheel almost grazed his windbreaker, and the air thundered behind it, echoing between the storefronts, when the engine was revved up.

"It's the dopers from the narco farm!"

Again Mik felt a compulsion to surrender. There was nothing else he could do. No matter what they did — whether they committed crimes or whether they bowed and said thank you very much — something was always wrong. Everything was going to go wrong in the end!

Here he stood in front of a raging superior force, a gang of huge grown-up men in creepy uniforms on giant machines, who were only out to catch him and beat him up. There was nothing left to do but throw himself to his knees and beg for mercy. If it wasn't the bikers it would have been the police. High above the noise of the motorcycles the burglar alarm was still wailing. There was no way out.

With the wheel in front of him and the headlight in his face, Mik backed up against the wall. He scraped his back on the bricks and tried to edge away, to get out of range, to bore into the wall itself — and suddenly there was a hole. The passageway! There was a gap between two buildings, there was a hole, there was darkness. It was like a vacuum, as if a sluice was suddenly opened up. As he stumbled backwards into the blackness, he saw that, just like the whirlpool around the drain of a kitchen sink, he was pulling Niels and the Shadow along with him. They ran backwards, tried to turn around, falling over each other and their own feet, the Shadow's long sleeves flapping like a scarecrow in the wind. They heard the motorcycles' rumble increase to a roar of rage, and one of the machines tried to come after them in the narrow gap but there obviously wasn't enough room; the light from its headlights flickered, and the engine emitted a tortured whine in neutral, while its back wheel spun around uselessly in thin air. They heard curses, but the sound of them fell farther back as the boys ran and bumped into hedges, broke through fences, stumbled, tore their skin on branches and thorns, got new rips in their jackets, but kept on running and running until they felt like their lungs were bursting and were going to crawl out of their mouths along with their hearts, running until at last they collapsed and had no idea where they were.

Except for the sound of their gasping breath it was surprisingly quiet. For some reason they lay close together, holding on to each other. They hadn't done it consciously; it just happened that way. Mik thought that this was the first time he had touched the Shadow — except for the time he was standing on his shoulders. It wasn't very often he touched Niels either. But he had been up climbing too. For a moment he enjoyed the security, then the problems came back. What was going to happen now?

"We've got to get out of here," said the Shadow. "Either they track us down or else the pigs will come after us. Either way we wind up in the joint, and I can't take it anymore."

"The 'joint'," whispered Niels, "what's that?"

"A detox center."

"I don't understand."

The Shadow's lenses gleamed. "What kind of hicks are you two, anyway?"

It wasn't as if he expected an answer. He just lay there a while. Then he said, "You mean you haven't ever been on the needle?"

"The needle?"

Suddenly the Shadow sat up, nervous.

"God, I don't feel like talking to you at all. It doesn't matter anyway. Now we're really up shit creek." He slapped himself on the forehead. "How could I be so goddamn stupid?"

They looked at him in the dark. He wasn't very big, but his jacket was way too big for him. And his hat.

"We've got to get going." He took off his hat and scratched at his red hair that stood straight up. "When the cops finally get moving, they'll be after us with dogs and everything."

Mik sat up. His hands were all scratched up, and now one sleeve of his windbreaker hung fluttering with a big rip in it. They must have looked awful.

"But where are we going to go?"

"To the city, of course, that's the only damn place you can be left in peace, isn't it?"

A little later he added, rather sadly, "If you can even be left in peace there."

Mik realized that they didn't even know the Shadow's name. Maybe it was a strange time to ask, but since everything was so weird anyway he might as well ask now.

"What's your name?"

"Who, me?" The Shadow looked at Mik suspiciously. "It doesn't make any difference, does it?"

But a little later he said: "Lars Kaj . . . Lars Kaj Jensen." It sounded as though it was hard for him to say it. As though he had said it many times when he didn't want to.

"Yeah but . . . we don't have any money. How are we going to . . . get to the city?" Niels sat up too, brushing dirt from his knees.

"We'll hitch in."

"What?"

The Shadow made a motion with his hand, circling his thumb in the air.

"Oh." Niels shook his head. "You get chased off down on the big highway. We were . . ."

"Yeah, there are cops all over the place. But if you get picked up by a car before it drives up on the freeway, then there's a chance. Of course there aren't very many people who stop, but once in a while . . . and we sure can't keep lying around here."

"But isn't it too dark?" Mik asked.

"Are you scared of the dark?"

Mik had never thought about it, but maybe he was. "Naw," he said uncertainly.

Lars Kaj got to his feet. "I don't know who you are, and nobody should ask too many questions anyway. But now we're mixed up together in this mess, so we'd better stick together."

Again his voice dropped, and he seemed sad. Maybe *he* was really the one who was afraid of the dark. Annoyed, he kicked the dirt.

"That's a bunch of crap. Actually the best thing is to be alone."

"Would you rather be . . . alone?" Mik asked softly.

"I usually am. I'm always alone. That's why I took off from the loony bin too. I couldn't stand the others."

"But . . ." said Niels. He didn't get any farther. The other two stared at him. All of a sudden he looked as if he was too big for his clothes — as if he had suddenly grown and couldn't fit inside himself anymore. He seemed lost.

"We don't even know where we are." He was whispering.

"It's 60 kilometers to Copenhagen," said the Shadow.

"Sixty kilometers?" It was 60 kilometers from their summer house to Copenhagen too. But they weren't anywhere near the summer house; it was almost as if it had never existed. All at once Mik felt that it was necessary for him to do something too, start thinking, make a plan.

"What if . . ." he said.

The other two looked at him.

"Don't you think it would be better . . . I mean, wouldn't it be hard to stop a car tonight? And if they're all out looking for us anyway, wouldn't it be better to stay somewhere nearby and hide out and then early tomorrow morning . . . try to get a lift?"

Lars Kaj looked pensive. Niels still looked just as lost as before.

"We'll never get home," he mumbled.

All this talk about "home" seemed to bother the Shadow. At any rate he turned to Niels and said, "You're always talking about 'home.' I don't know what you're talking about. I don't have any goddamn 'home.' I split years ago. You can't trip out and have a home too. If you're on the needle, you don't have any home — except maybe a detox center. But it's obviously no use talking to you two about it. You don't understand shit."

"Do you?" asked Mik, surprised at his own anger. "You don't even answer my questions."

The Shadow stood there a while thinking. His face had disappeared again in the darkness. Then he nodded.

"OK, man," he said. "Maybe it is better for us to keep a low profile until tomorrow. But where the hell are we going to go?"

"Can't we sleep in a haystack?"

"And get a Doberman up our ass? Anyway, there aren't any haystacks. I thought you were the ones who were hicks. And you don't even know that the hay is harvested in June. I learned *something* in the flippo factory at least."

He seemed annoyed.

"Haystacks. There aren't any haystacks! There haven't been any haystacks for years. What the hell are you babbling about now? You're going to drive me nuts."

"Isn't there a river?"

"A river? What do we need a river for?"

Niels got excited. "If there's a river or even a creek, we

could walk in it a ways, and then the dogs will lose the scent, so they can't find us if the cops... if they come with the dogs!"

The Shadow whistled between his teeth. Then he looked at Niels with respect.

"Not bad, boss. I hadn't thought of that one before."

Niels had gotten his old voice back. "Maybe you never read books," he said, with a touch of superiority.

"No, God knows I don't. But if that's the kind of thing that's in books, then I'd better get going. And there is a river, by the way. But it's on the other side of town... away from Copenhagen."

Niels had gotten more excited after his success. "Don't you see, that's better yet! If they think we got away, then they'll search in the direction of the city, won't they?"

"I guess so."

"And then we'll have a head start!"

Already it seemed that the plan they were now working on was far more important than how they were ever going to get home. Without a plan, of course, they wouldn't have a chance.

They couldn't hear the siren of the burglar alarm anymore, and only once in a while did a vague rumbling tell them that the motorcycles were still riding around in the streets.

"So we'll try that," said the Shadow, nodding, "but it'll be a hell of a steeplechase. We'll have to go around the whole town and not set foot in it."

"What if the guys on the motorcycles ride out here... what if they're spreading out?"

"Oh, they aren't so tough. They won't spread out, that's

for sure. They always ride together. And when they start getting bored they don't feel like it anymore. By tomorrow they'll forget all about us. But the cops, that's another story. They hate us."

"They hate us?"

"Well, not you guys. You're just a couple of candyasses. But me." He said it with a mixture of bitterness and pride. "I'm a subversive, after all. That's what you are when you take drugs. Then you cost money, society's money, taxpayers' money, and they hate you."

He looked around quickly. "That's why we'd better see about getting our asses in gear."

He shoved his hat down on his head. "When we get to the city our chances will be better."

In the dark he looked like a little troll dressed up like a fine gentleman. He turned toward them.

"If the whole shithole doesn't blow up in our face, that is."

He stood on the edge of a furrow and looked a little taller. A glow along the horizon outlined his silhouette.

"What do you mean?" asked Mik.

"War . . . that's all they're blabbing about."

"War? But I thought it was peacetime! I thought the war was over . . ."

"Which war?"

"*The* war."

"I don't know what you're talking about."

"There was war in . . . 1941," Mik stammered.

"In 1941? I can't remember that . . . oh, *that* war, the one with that Hitler guy. That was sometime in the middle ages or whenever it was. Yeah, that one's over."

"Well, then what?"

"Then nothing. There's just been war ever since."

"A world war?"

"Well, you couldn't really call it that, but there's been war all over the world. Korea, Vietnam, the Middle East, Iran, Afghanistan, Pakistan, El Salvador . . . and all those other places. And now it looks like *everything's* going to hell."

"But I thought . . ."

"What'd you think?"

Mik didn't know what to say, and he almost didn't dare ask the question: Was it the Germans who won?

His outlook on the world had been turned upside down so many times that he couldn't make heads or tails of it. Here he sat on the edge of a garden next to a plowed field, and everything that had been more or less clear to him before: England against Germany, the Nazis against the Communists, the loyalists against the rebels in Spain, the Japanese against the Chinese, the Poles against the Germans, all that was suddenly gone and replaced by other wars and conflicts in countries he hardly knew the names of. The Finns, whom they had heard so much about, were not even mentioned now. It was terrifying and totally incomprehensible.

"Who won?" he asked softly.

"Who won what? Shit, nobody won a thing."

"But the Germans . . . the Germans back then?"

"Oh, sure, they got whipped. There wasn't a brick left standing."

Mik felt a vague relief. The enemy had been whipped! He glanced over at Niels, who was sitting hunched up, looking the other way. It was inconceivable that he wouldn't be interested in this. Maybe he thought the whole thing was a dream. Or else he was so hungry that he couldn't even listen.

"So why should there be war," Mik said quite loudly, "if the Germans were beaten?"

Lars Kaj put a finger to his temple and rotated it several times.

"The Germans! You keep talking about the Germans. What the hell has it got to do with them? You're totally full of shit!"

He looked around. "But I think this is a weird time to be holding a political discussion. We were just trying to break into a laundromat, and in two minutes the panzers will be on our tail, and we're sitting here bullshitting. We're pissing around like a bunch of amateurs. Are you coming?"

"Yeah," said Mik. He wanted to go.

He wanted to go, not just because they had to get away from the police, but because he also felt a compulsion to find out more. His insides were swirling around. Now he had not only reached a line that he could push back and forth at will and maybe even step over — now he was up to his ears in something that was totally incomprehensible, something that was so complicated that he couldn't conceive of it.

But somewhere at the edge of his heart he felt a warm ripple. Naturally he couldn't say that he knew the Shadow. They'd been together for what, two hours? Still he felt the same vibrating consent with him that he felt with Niels, no matter how much they disagreed or how much they argued and teased each other. Lars Kaj was a total stranger, and half of what he said was impossible to understand. But he was a boy, they shared that at least, and Mik felt that he might also become a friend.

They all got to their feet. Leaning over, they began to run in an arc southwest around the town, so that they could reach the river and find a place where they could hide until it got light and the chances of getting to the city were better.

6

Suddenly the creek was in front of them. It was a surprise, both because it was dark and because there were no rushes. Here it ran straight through a field, and if the Shadow hadn't had a hunch, they would have gone head over heels off the embankment. Now they lay down carefully on their stomachs and slipped down until they could hear the soft, rushing sound of the water. Mik took a sniff. It didn't smell the way it used to at Ramløse Creek. He had seen creeks before where rushes didn't grow, and even though there were a lot of them growing where Ramløse Creek runs into the Arresø, he was ready to concede that not all creeks were the same. But the smell! It was the same smell he remembered from the cave, when they came out through the hole with the spinning colors. The sudden, acrid odor that stung your nose and made your guts cramp a little. He had hold of Niels' sleeve, and they were sitting next to each other on the bank of the creek. In the dusk they couldn't see very much, but still they had gotten used to the darkness enough so that the creek almost looked like a strip of light. It might be the current and the bubbles in it, but it still seemed odd that the stream could give off so much light.

"OK, let's get our feet moving," said the Shadow. He was already busy taking off his shoes and socks.

"What's that smell?" whispered Niels.

"What smell? Or do you think my toes are funky? Just because I'm a drugged-out wreck doesn't mean I can't take care of my personal hygiene."

"But it stinks!"

Lars Kaj turned to Niels. "All right, you, don't start in on me!"

Mik broke in. "He means the creek — the water — it smells so weird here."

"It does?" The Shadow looked around, feigning surprise. "Does it smell especially weird here? That's how all creeks smell, don't they?"

Niels didn't quite catch his irony. "Sure, creeks might smell a little, of decay and mud, but they don't smell like this."

Lars Kaj stood with his shoes and socks in his hand.

"I don't know where the hell you're from, but whatever smells in that creek is the same thing most other creeks smell like. It starts with a P and it's called pollution."

Mik sat with his shoe halfway off. The creek running through Frederiksværk had foam on it once. But he had never seen a creek that was totally white from "pollution."

"Where does it come from?"

"Well, there's a paper mill farther up a ways, and then

there are two chemical plants a couple of kilometers south of here. And the fields, of course."

"The fields? said Niels. "What's wrong with the fields?"

"Actually I should be getting paid for this," muttered the Shadow. "But it's like this, ladies and gents: they spray the fields with all kinds of chemicals and shit to kill the insects and so-called pests, and then when it rains, all the poison washes off, and it has to go somewhere, and since the soil tilts toward the creek the way it's supposed to, all the shit runs into the creek. So, does anybody want to go wading? It was your idea, after all."

He went down the creek bank and stepped into the foaming water. Standing there like a miniature Old Testament prophet, he turned toward the two boys, stretched out his arms, and said, "There's one thing you can be thankful for, anyway. You'll never get your toe bitten by a pike, because there hasn't been a fish alive in this water for the last ten years."

About a kilometer to the west they found a place where they could cross the creek, and when they had crawled up the other side they lay down for a while to dry their legs and put their shoes back on. Their pants were wet quite a ways up, but only Niels had fallen into a hole and gotten wet above his waist.

A thin layer of clouds, which had covered the sky since shortly after sundown, gradually moved toward the east, and the stars came out across the entire vault of the heavens. Mik stared at them and experienced a feeling of continuity. Everything seemed changed — he had felt sick to his stomach when they waded through the chemical foam in the creek, which

had crept up his legs and clung in slimy clumps of bubbles —
but here was a connection, here he saw a recognizable order
that apparently reigned in every age. He had gotten dizzy
when he stood outside the summer house in the evening and
looked up at the Milky Way. Even then it was with a feeling,
at once shivering and safe, that even if there had been other
times and other times were to come, there was still a continuity, a continuity throughout all eternity, you might say.

He tried to concentrate on the great calm. And he suc-
ceeded for a while. There was a moment when he forgot the
hunger and the exhaustion and the worries about all the
things he didn't understand that had happened to him, but
then he noticed that beneath the starry sky his nervousness
still quivered. He thought about his father and mother and his
sister. How could he help it? How was he supposed to go
about forgetting them, the people who filled his entire existence, the ones he knew felt the same way about him? He
imagined how they were searching, how they were moving
heaven and earth to find him, how worried they all were —
Niels' parents too, and Anna and his big brother Ole. It was
well past midnight now, and Mik felt convinced that none of
them were sleeping a wink. Maybe his mother and father had
put on their nightclothes — they would have forced his sister
to go to bed, anyway, "so she at least could get a little sleep."
They themselves were no doubt sitting in the living room, or
over at Mr. and Mrs. Storm's, talking with them. There must
have been a bulletin — and the police must have been noti-
fied. In his short life Mik had never had any direct contact
with the police. Now he was both listed as missing and on the

run! His life took place on two levels, which were flowing together in his mind so that he couldn't tell them apart. The picture of the helmeted constables he was used to seeing in his early childhood was merging with the picture of the monstrous, swaying helicopter with the voice that had shouted at him through a loudspeaker. He was sure there weren't any constables sitting in it, even if it did belong to the police.

He tried to concentrate on the starry sky in order to calm down again. With his eyes wide open he located the well-known constellations: the Big Dipper, the Pleiades, Orion's Belt, the Little Bear and the Great Bear, but then he saw that the stars were moving! He blinked his eyes and opened them wide again. It couldn't be a shooting star, as he first thought. The speed was wrong, and the shining star moved in an arc the way you imagined all stars did, only more slowly, when they glided across the sky on their normal paths. A little later he discovered that it wasn't just one star that was moving. There were a lot of them. They were sailing back and forth and criss-crossing too. So even the universe wasn't stable any longer, the firmament itself had started to dissolve.

Mik felt a shiver run through his entire body. He had read about the big comet whose path might someday cross the orbit of the earth and crush it, but he had never expected it to happen during his lifetime, or ever, for that matter. He had seen shooting stars in the black August nights and closed his eyes and secretly made a wish for something good, the way he knew you could, and there had been a real solar eclipse during his lifetime, when he and his big sister had stood out on the road with tinted glass in front of their eyes and looked at the unnaturally glowing disk covered by the shadow of the moon. But wandering stars so close and so bright—that had to mean something special.

He had totally forgotten Niels' wet shorts and his own cold toes while he had this strange experience. He was so engrossed that he almost didn't dare ask what it was he was seeing. A huge shadow loomed over him—and they had already asked about so many things anyway. Everything seemed to contain question marks; everything they got close to was new and different. He had to find out, or else he wouldn't be able to stand it.

"Lars Kaj," he said.

The Shadow was sitting in his oversized jacket, struggling with his socks.

"They always come out ten sizes too small after they put them in the dryer up at the joint. Shit." He gave up and looked at Mik. "What is it?"

Mik pointed up into the darkness. "That . . . up in the sky . . . what is it?"

Lars Kaj made a disgusted face. "Now really, I don't feel like playing this guessing game with you anymore. The first thing you know, you'll be asking me which is up and which is down, your head or your ass."

"But there's something moving up there. Some of the stars are moving." Niels was staring up at the sky too.

"Satellites," said the Shadow, and continued trying to squeeze his feet into his socks.

"What did you say?"

"Satellites. Communications satellites, spy satellites, weather satellites. Yeah, now they even have fully-armed nuclear satellites zooming around up there too, I guess, so what else is new?"

They didn't say a word. But they didn't understand a thing either. Lars Kaj glared at them.

"Why don't you ever tell *me* anything? Why am I always the one who has to give a lecture? What are you, spies or something?" His eyes opened wider. "Is that what you are? Just somebody the cops sent out to set me up? Police informants, is that what you are? Jesus Christ . . ."

The Shadow got up. Then he suddenly started to run.

Terrified, Mik jumped to his feet.

"Lars Kaj," he shouted, "Lars Kaj!"

If their new friend disappeared, they were lost. He sensed that right away. So he started running after him, faster than he thought possible, because he only had one shoe on.

"Lars Kaj, Lars Kaj!"

He was going so fast that he didn't even notice that the Shadow had stopped until he crashed into him, and they both tumbled over in the dark.

"You crazy shit," hissed Lars Kaj. "If you keep on yelling like that, our good looks will be history."

They lay side by side for a while, gasping. Then Mik said, "You won't even believe us if we tell you who we are."

He listened to his own breathing. How was he going to get the Shadow to believe the story about the cave and the ruins, which evidently were located in a completely different place — in a completely different time. He *couldn't* explain it, and if he started in on it, his friend would think it was a lie. He had to think of something.

In the dark no one could see that he was blushing, but he

did when he said, almost inaudibly, "We ran away from home."

The Shadow had no reaction; he just lay there, not moving.

"We . . . we couldn't work it out with our parents. So we ran away from home."

His throat constricted because he couldn't help thinking about his mother and father when he told the lie. All at once he remembered Niels and missed him. He was probably unhappy alone in the dark. Mik sat up and yelled, "Niels, Niels!"

Suddenly he felt a hand over his mouth and his head being forced backwards. It was the Shadow again.

"Are you totally out of your mind?" he hissed. "Can you try and keep your trap shut, or are you anxious to take a trip to the nut house? Or wherever they put guys like you."

In the dark they made out Niels' outline as he approached. He plopped down beside them. Without saying anything, all three of them sat there for a while. They were all in this together, but at the same time they were each independent too. Mik felt that they could solve certain problems, but there were things nobody would help them with that they had to manage by themselves.

"I'm not a spy," said Niels.

"No, so I hear." The Shadow had lain down on his back. "Anyway, I don't care."

There was a hint of defeat in his voice that they hadn't heard before. "I don't give a damn about any of this."

They waited for him to continue. Earlier he had been full of energy, but now he lay there as if he was burnt out.

"We might as well just walk on back. At least you'd get yourselves something to eat. They always make sure that you get something to eat, so it doesn't really matter what you did."

"But you said —"

"What'd I say?"

"You said that . . . they beat you."

"Did I say that? The only thing I probably said was that they were assholes."

Mik sighed. "I have to go back and get my shoe."

He sat up and stared into the darkness. Niels' face was glowing white, and he noticed that it must be the reflection of dawn breaking. It was already almost daylight. A new nervousness took hold of him.

"But look, Niels has money. That was why we ran away, that's the reason we're on the road. We're supposed to go into the city, wasn't that what you said?"

"Yeah, sure."

Mik wrung his hands and stared up at the sky, so that it looked for a moment as if he was praying to God. The stars kept speeding by in huge arcs. Some of them seemed even clearer than before, as though they wanted to prove that they were brighter than the dawn.

"When it gets light, can you see them then too?"

The Shadow looked at him. "Do they take the stars in during the day where you come from?"

Life had returned to the Shadow's voice again. "If you weren't so idiotic that you almost make me cry, I would have died laughing long ago." He sat up. "You probably even think they park the moon somewhere in the daytime so the people running around up there fall off and float around somewhere in space."

"There aren't any people on the moon," Niels said suddenly in a loud, firm voice.

The Shadow looked at him in surprise. "No, for once you're right. There's probably nobody up there at the moment. They're too busy with all their shit everywhere else to be able to deal with the moon right now. But they *have* been there, believe me. There isn't anywhere these days where *homo sapiens* hasn't planted his smelly feet. And what have we got out of it? Well, from the moon I think it was a bag of eight hundred pounds of broken rock, but I haven't heard about anything else. *Homo sapiens* — give me a break."

"Have *people* been on the moon?"

The Shadow shook his head. "I don't know where you've been hiding out the last twenty years. It couldn't have been in this neck of the woods."

"Answer me," Niels said firmly.

"You can hear what I'm saying, can't you! People *have* been on the moon, and people are riding around up there right now too." He pointed at the lightening sky. "There have been probes and spaceships on Mars and Venus, they discovered a gas cloud, whatever the hell that is, that's millions of times bigger than the galaxy we live in . . . Well, I don't know why I'm sitting here talking like a professor about something I don't know shit about, but you keep asking, and it's driving me nuts. Shall we go?"

The summer light arrived more quickly than they had thought it would. From a pale gray shadow in the north it spread toward the east, and along with the light came the cold. They suddenly noticed how wet and miserable they were. And the hunger, which had been forgotten, began creeping back into their stomachs. The Shadow was right. The best thing was to keep moving. Maybe it was already too late; they should have been near the big highway by now, before the police started putting an all-points bulletin into effect. What if they did? Would they really come looking for three boys who hadn't done much more than open a window?

Mik had put on his shoes and socks. He looked over at Niels. When they started moving he would feel even colder, but then the warmth would come. The best thing was to get going.

They ran alongside the grain field, and when they came to a dirt crossroad they turned off and followed it a ways, even though it was probably leading them back toward the town, but it was heading in the direction of the big highway too. The buildings were different here than when the boys had first approached the town. Many of the buildings looked like small factories or workshops, and there were gas stations with banners strung up and fluttering gently in the morning breeze. From the top of a fencepost a finch sang its early-morning descending trill, and as he walked briskly onward Mik thought: There is a bird after all! It seemed like a paradox, but when he thought about it, he missed the birds just as much as he missed his mother and father. That couldn't be right, but when he heard the finch in the morning dawn, he knew that a world without birds would be impossible for him to live in.

Suddenly the Shadow stopped and held up one arm as a sign for them to wait. His face was now quite visible, and Mik saw the alert eyes behind his glasses and the clearly drawn furrows running from both sides of his nose down past the corners of his mouth. Lars Kaj was listening intently. He might have looked like a hunting dog that has picked up a scent and stopped frozen in his tracks, but he was much too clumsy in that baggy coat and a wide-brimmed hat that only a preacher would wear. As though it was an echo and not the sound itself, they could hear the barking of a dog far away. It might be any old dog, or it might be *the dogs*. They had no idea, and even the Shadow couldn't be sure. They were standing on a little hilltop where the road made a bend, and the Shadow crooked his finger and motioned them forward. He touched Niels' shoulder and turned him around so he was facing in the direction of the nearest gas station. Lars Kaj raised his arm. Mik looked in that direction. In front of the white building with the gas pumps and the waving banners stood four cars. They were parked a little to one side, and even at this distance they could see that there were pieces of paper on the windshields with something written on them. The Shadow squatted down and pulled Niels down with him. Mik did the same.

"Are you with me?" whispered Lars Kaj.

They answered with quizzical looks.

He shook his head in disgust. "We're going to appropriate a car!"

Mik wanted to say something, but the Shadow hushed him with a finger to his lips.

"I'll take care of it. But we have to plan the tactics. We can't just walk up to the lot, all three of us. You two have to sneak in first. Walk down the road, then I'll hot-wire the old crate, and if I can get the piece of shit to work then I'll come down the road like a bat out of hell, and then you jump in. Got it?"

"Sure, but . . ." whispered Niels, "you don't even have a driver's license!"

For an instant it looked like the Shadow was going to drop the whole thing and lie down on the road and go to sleep. Then he raised his hands to heaven and rolled his eyes.

"Goddamn it to hell," he hissed, "didn't you hear what I said? We're starting to walk *now,* and when I turn off, you just keep going straight ahead, OK? You just tippytoe on down the road, and then I'll show up — if I can, and then we'll have to hustle our buns."

They both nodded, and all three of them started off in the direction of the gas station. There was a little sound from Niels' shorts every time he took a step. The wet black edges on the inside were scraping against each other. It was a strange march. Mik suddenly thought that every time they did something that was going to get them out of trouble, they automatically did something else illegal. Maybe that's what it was like being a criminal — and a fugitive. Maybe it had always been like that, but in the world he was in now it almost seemed to be the rule. They had hardly emerged from the burial mound before they had done something forbidden. Maybe just going down in the cave was against the law. Mik had had a secret, and from the moment he decided to make use of it, everything went wrong. He felt challenged by the thought. Was there only law and order in the world or the opposite: crime, pursuit, flight, and punishment? That couldn't be true — but as he followed out of the corner of his eye the

Shadow's quick, crouching figure running up toward the parked cars, he couldn't help wishing that it would go well, that he would be able to start the car so they could get away from here and be saved.

The words "get away" kept ringing in his ears as he walked side by side with Niels along the sidewalk. If they got away, they would automatically get farther away from their starting point! And then how would they find their way back? It would be impossible to come near this little town ever again. Here both the police and the men in the black leather clothes with the motorcycles would be waiting for them. Never before had Mik felt that things were always set up so that you couldn't have one thing without having to accept its opposite at the same time. Here he was, walking and walking in short pants beside his friend as the sun shone a fan of pink searchlights up over a clump of low clouds that had formed on the horizon, and at the same time his other "friend" was about to try starting a car . . . in order to steal it! It was almost impossible to take in.

He glanced out of the corner of his eye and turned his head halfway around and saw that the Shadow had gotten the hood up on a black car and was leaning over with his head down in the engine. Mik thought about how often he had dreamed about driving a car, how delicious the feeling was when it happened in his dreams. It was no effort, he didn't have to exert himself, everything just proceeded naturally. He sat behind the wheel and only needed to turn it a little before the car would start moving. That's how it really felt, he knew, because he sat up front with Jens Ewald when they drove up to the summer house, and all of them were there, and the yellow wicker trunk was tied on tight behind. He couldn't help feeling excited at the thought that maybe he would be riding in his own car soon — even though it wasn't his.

He hadn't finished his train of thought when two sounds at the same time broke over him and Niels. The two sounds were actually one: the car engine starting and the hood being slammed. They saw Lars Kaj jump like a big crow in one hop from in front of the car to behind the steering wheel, and all at once a new sound was let loose. It was a dog barking, and it must have been a big dog, because it was almost drowning out the sound of the engine as the Shadow raced it until it roared. Without thinking, Niels and Mik edged a little closer to each other. They knew that they ought to start running now, that they had to be moving to be able to jump in as Lars Kaj drove by, but they were so entranced by what was happening that all at once they couldn't move, they were so excited.

The black car stood still for a moment, as if with all its horsepower and its tremendous roar it had to overcome an invisible barrier, then it sprang loose and lurched forward, just as the metal door to one of the garages was pushed up with a rumble, and the dog appeared, with a man in pajamas next to him. He had the dog on a leash, but it was so wild that he couldn't hold it back — or else he didn't want to. Anyway, the dog got loose, and while the Shadow maneuvered between the gas pumps in a roar of acceleration toward the driveway, the dog crouched down and then leaped up against the car windows with its jaws gaping and its tongue flapping in a frenzy of barking.

Mik felt like they were frozen solid to the pavement. Now it wasn't a dream anymore, and even though it was difficult, he tore himself free and shouted to Niels: "Come on, come on!"

His friend turned his head anxiously, as if he wanted to say: I can't, I can't! Then he started running too, and from behind they heard the sound of the car, which came tearing out of the gas station with tires screeching, heading toward them and the big concrete highway farther down the road. They both tried to look ahead and behind them simultaneously, but time was running out, because along with the sound of the car's engine they could hear the dog's terrible barking and knew that it was on their heels. The man in the pajamas had also started to run, but he stopped when he reached the road.

At that instant the black car came up beside Niels and Mik. Through the windshield they could see the Shadow's face bouncing up and down as he tried to steer the car, brake, and get the doors open at the same time, so the others would have a chance to jump in.

Then there was the dog. It had first concentrated on the original thief, but then it caught sight of Niels and Mik and turned its attention to them. It seemed to elongate, to stretch out, to assume the shape of its own speed; it stretched its head forward and lifted its legs high, it closed its mouth, and its eyes were wild. Then the dog put on more speed, and if they had seen it from the side it would have looked like a black streak in the air. But they saw mostly its head and its glowing eyes and its mouth, which was soon open again, tongue sticking out, jaws snapping. At the same instant that Mik felt its moist breath on the back of his leg, he also saw a swinging car door and tried to grab hold, to clamp onto it, then his feet were out from under him and he just hung in the air and had to fight with all his might not to fall off again. His legs were flung back and forth, supernatural forces seemed to be pulling at his arms, and as he hung there he saw that Niels had grabbed hold of the edge of the back door, which was also flapping, but then they heard the Shadow yell, "Are you in? Are you in?" But they couldn't say anything because they had to use all their strength to hang on, and the hound's snout and wet canine teeth were still right between them. Then Lars Kaj speeded up and the pavement turned into an insane black band disappearing beneath them. Niels was inside; he slammed the door shut and might have caught the dog in it, because it let out a howl, turned a couple of somersaults, and started running again, but Niels had hold of Mik's arm, and as the car weaved from side to side, picking up speed, Mik got inside and felt how he was starting to shake all over, as if he was getting sick and had caught a fever. He threw himself back onto the seat, and even though he was sitting in front, it wasn't like riding with Jens Ewald, it was totally different, and he didn't know if he ever wanted to try it again.

"What's happening?" yelled Lars Kaj. "What happened to the old fart?"

Niels turned around and looked out the window. Mik was still lying awkwardly across the seat, gasping for breath and trying to recover.

"He stopped — and now he's going back. He's running!"

"Hold onto your hats," wailed the Shadow, stomping even harder on the gas. "Now we've got to move our butts!"

From his reclining position Mik noticed how the violent weaving began to diminish as their speed increased. At the same time he felt the hard-soft rubberlike material of the seat covers against his skin. It had a harsh, chemical smell. Shadows were whizzing by over his head, and when he raised himself to a half-upright position he saw a series of blue signs with white letters fly past. He caught the name "Copenhagen" — but it also said "Helsingør." He couldn't figure out a double white cross standing on end, but now the Shadow yelled again.

"Here's the freeway — hold on!"

Suddenly he braked hard, and Mik had to lean back hard so that he wouldn't slide across the front seat. Right afterward they were flung over to the left side of the car, and Lars Kaj shoved his leg against Mik to keep him away from the wheel. The car went into a violent fishtail again, but just as Mik thought they would fly off the edge of the shoulder with the cloud of gravel and rocks spraying around them, the rear wheels got a grip on the pavement again — they must be on the concrete highway already. And with the gas pedal jammed to the floor they shot like a rocket onto the huge roadway, divided in three, that Mik and Niels had seen from the side the day before.

The words kept ringing in Mik's mind: "The day before." His sense of time had been shattered to such an extent that he might as well have called it last year or ten years ago or forty-seven. He had gone through more in the last twenty-four hours than in his entire life, and even when he thought of the day the Germans came, and another time, when he and Niels had seen an adder and later it had been killed and had fifteen live baby snakes inside, all of that seemed like nothing compared to what was happening now. The peculiar pressure in his heart he had noticed earlier came back. Forty-seven years! Could forty-seven years really have passed in a day or two? It was impossible, even though he had heard stories about people suddenly about to die reliving their whole life in a few seconds. But his feeling wasn't like that. The time from when they went into the cave until now was real, he was sure of that. He could see each and every event clearly before him, even when he lay as he did now and was actually in a new situation that demanded his undivided attention.

But basically there was no difference. He couldn't separate the events, and yet each was distinct. When he thought things through they lay jumbled on top of each other: the man in the field, the bakery lady, his mother, Anna, the man in leather, the family in front of the television set, the dog. He could think about them together or one at a time. Through the bottom of the car he could hear the sound of the tires on the pavement, a rumbling whine that was chopped to bits by rhythmic bumps where the pieces of the roadway must be fitted together. Everything was new, but suddenly it seemed to him that he had been familiar with all this for his entire life. It was a mysterious sensation, for when he thought back to the time before the cave, he had no idea about the existence of all this. But now he felt that it must have been living somewhere inside him as a feeling, a possibility, a thought, or a dream. Maybe he had wished for it so hard that the whole thing became reality — but before that thought was quite complete in his head, he rejected it. This wasn't what he wanted!

Through the window he saw the countryside, which was now bright and clear in the early morning sunshine. It was green and starting to turn yellow, the harvest was approaching, and it looked like country he had seen before. But something was different: everywhere he saw tall masts and poles, high-tension lines dipped down over the fields or off to the horizon on their huge towers. But what bothered him most were the towns scattered around here and there. They looked so random and shabby, the paint seemed artificial, the buildings were all too similar, built of the same kind of wood, or gray and yellow bricks. But the worst thing was the roofs, flat and black, as if the buildings had pulled a coffin lid over themselves and were waving for help with the thin fingers of the television antennas — they had to be television antennas, after what he had seen.

Mik turned toward the Shadow, who sat bent intently over the wheel, staring out the windshield through his fragile welfare glasses. Mik could see now that the lenses were thick. Lars Kaj must be nearsighted. It made him feel more kindly toward him. Mik heaved a sigh. It was terribly exhausting, not just what they had been through, but this sensation of the doubleness of everything. Just as he sat there despising the countryside and its whole atmosphere, he caught sight of the Shadow's thick glasses and felt his heart beat in a different way. Now it was far from contempt he felt, more an amazement that you could be fond of someone, even though you had lost almost everything you loved most and were riding along a totally alien concrete highway, zooming through a hostile landscape at ninety miles an hour. Mik had never ridden in a car going this fast, but here on the big road it didn't seem so awfully fast. It was almost a little reassuring after the violent swerving and skidding at the start of the ride. You could almost fall asleep.

It was ages since Mik had stayed up all night. He had no idea what time it was; it had to be at least three or four. Oh, the way he used to keep nagging for permission to stay up late! He did it almost every evening, but he was called in as early as nine o'clock, or nine-thirty in the summer. Usually when they were playing — and often when they were having the most fun — he would hear his mother's voice: "Mik . . . Mikkel! You come home right now!" He was sure that no one was calling now, at least not his mother.

"If we keep up this pace it'll take less than an hour to reach the city," said the Shadow. "If there's enough gas in this crate, that is, and we don't fall into some radar trap."

"What's that?"

"Oh God," said Lars Kaj. He put his hand over his eyes for a moment, but not long enough to make Mik really nervous. "I've tried to get used to it, and I also decided not to overreact when you guys ask your stupid questions. I said to myself: Lars Kaj, just answer. It's no use anyway."

There was no denying he knew a lot of words, a lot more than Niels and Mik did.

"A radar trap — let's see, a radar trap, well, it's a thing sort of like . . . No, goddamn it, it just won't work, I'll have to start at the beginning."

So then the Shadow told them about bats and their supersonic echo soundings, about radar screens and photoelectric cells, but even though both Niels and Mik understood the words, they still thought that what they heard was fantastic and almost incomprehensible — and totally logical at the same time. So now they had to start being afraid of a radar trap. It seemed as though the demands on them were piling up minute by minute.

At this hour of the morning the highway was still empty. They watched the dotted lines coming toward them, and when they saw them flashing by the hood of the car, it was obvious that they were driving very fast. Now and then a sign at the side of the road would whiz past, and there was no doubt that the number 60 meant that you weren't supposed to drive any faster than that. Lars Kaj paid no attention to it, and why should he? They were already involved in so many things that one more law ignored wouldn't tip the scales much.

Little by little, drowsiness began to take hold of Mik. It was the same rhythm all the time, the same view to the left and right. The road never changed, it just cut straight ahead — straight forward the way they were going and straight back. Just before he closed his eyes and slipped into a kind of semi-consciousness, where the sound of the wheels and the engine flowed together in a faraway rumble, he saw that Niels had collapsed on the back seat and sat sleeping with his head on his knees.

But Mik didn't manage to drift off completely, because suddenly he heard the Shadow swearing, and when he opened his eyes he saw that the empty road in the oncoming direction was no longer empty. Heavy green vehicles were moving in a long column. They had their lights on, and some of them had long antennas sticking up, waving in the wind. At first they were soundless, but when they drew up opposite them the noise of their engines and the rumbling of their caterpillar treads increased until it was a compact thundering that made the dashboard of their own car vibrate.

"They're really moving," said Lars Kaj. "As far as I can see, half of them are German."

"But I thought the war was over!" Niels blurted out. He had also sat up when the new thundering broke loose. "You said it yourself. The Germans lost! Then how . . . how can they be driving around here?"

"Nothing to it. As you can see."

Niels shook his head. "So who's on whose side — and who's against who? I thought the Danes . . . that we . . ." He fell back, bewildered.

Mik tried to help him understand. He went over it in his mind: first it was the Germans against . . . almost the whole world. They were against the English and the French and the Poles and the Dutch and the Belgians and the Danes and the Norwegians. But they weren't against the Italians and the Japanese and the Russians. They were on the same side, well, maybe not on the same side as the Russians, but they had something called a non-aggression pact. Denmark had had one with the Germans too, but what good did that do? And now they were driving around in tanks on the Danish highways — and Mik couldn't see the difference between the Danish and the German tanks. Apparently there wasn't any difference.

"What about the Allies?" he asked cautiously.

"I don't know who the Allies are," said the Shadow. "It keeps changing. But we *are* a member of NATO."

"NATO?"

"Yeah, that's something called the North Atlantic Defense Organization or something like that. The Americans run the whole thing, but the Germans are right up there kissing the gold watch. They're the richest country in Europe!"

"So — they won after all," muttered Niels.

"Yeah, you could say that."

The military column on the opposite side of the road seemed endless. It rumbled along at a steady pace: first came the armored personnel carriers, then the regular tanks and the big flatbed trucks, again carrying those bombs propped up at an angle and sticking up in the air.

Niels pointed at one of them. "What's that?"

"Mobile rocket batteries. Maybe with nuclear warheads."

Things were starting to mount up again. No matter what they talked about, the heap of questions kept growing. What did all these strange terms mean? There was no way to keep everything straight, but one thing seemed obvious: it was all mysterious and it was all terrifying, in some way. Not just what they could see; both Niels and Mik were somewhat used to seeing a lot of military moving along the roads. It was more the unfathomable meaning of the words that seemed threatening. They were constantly hearing new words and terms that they didn't understand, and precisely because the terms were technical and incomprehensible, their significance grew and became aggressive and sinister. They had to get *something* straight; there had to be something to go by.

"Who are we against?" asked Mik tentatively.

The Shadow shrugged his shoulders. They almost reached as far as the edge of his broad-brimmed hat.

"Well, I guess it's the Russians," he said. "At least they're the ones the Americans are against. I don't know what side I'm on. I just want to be here . . . somehow."

"But is there a war on?"

Lars Kaj gave a strangely evasive answer. "A war on? There's war all the time. I think there's been war forever. At least as long as I've been alive. But now they're getting ready for the big one. I just don't feel like keeping up with it."

His words sounded depressing; the sight outside their window was hostile. Long black shadows seemed to fall from the sky, and the morning sun came out from behind the clouds. Their own war seemed idyllic in comparison; the black airplane flew over their roof every day, firing its machine guns, but it was just shooting at a target down on the beach. Of course there were other places . . . but they were far away. Now the trucks and cannons were driving right past their window. German and Danish together. Maybe there were more of them.

Mik turned around to see how long the column stretched in the other direction, but his gaze was distracted by something moving in the sky. At first it looked like just a black dot; when it came closer and he saw what it was, he grabbed Niels by the arm, hard. Both of them stared out the back window, and in a matter of seconds there was no doubt. It was the police helicopter! Before their eyes it grew from a black dot as it sped toward them up the cement highway. It was like an insect expanding and breaking out of a cocoon, which still hangs from it like an extra weight while the insect's wings flap in frenetic rage.

With a sucking sound the heavy aircraft caught up with them and descended to a low elevation above the pavement so that they could see the letters POLICE painted on the side and the men sitting in the glass cockpit with dark glasses and earphones on. The air pressure from the great windmill above the cockpit made their car swerve so much that Lars Kaj was forced to slow down. Still, he leaned over the steering wheel and held on tight with both hands, as if he was determined to keep from being swept off the road by this new threat that seemed so overwhelming.

The sound of the metallic voice from the loudspeakers on the helicopter pounded against their eardrums: "CS 62 881 — you have been identified. Pull over and stop immediately! This is the police."

The Shadow kept staring at the road ahead. Mik and Niels had their eyes glued to the aircraft, as huge as a locomotive hovering obliquely before them at seventy-five feet off the ground.

"Attention, attention! CS 62 881 — if you do not obey our orders we will have to take action. We repeat: CS 62 881 — this is your last chance. Pull over and stop."

The Shadow's glasses flashed. "You're bluffing," he shouted at the windshield toward the helicopter, "you chickenshits!"

He sped up again, and all at once the helicopter climbed, as though his raging outburst had had an effect. The boys stared at the maneuver in amazement, as the aircraft tipped forward some more and exposed its wheels and bracing wires and its bulging belly to them in a way that seemed almost indecent. Now what?

The explanation came a few seconds later, when the climbing maneuver was reversed: a thousand feet further down the road the helicopter landed. The pilot set it down in the center lane, and it looked like a ballet dancer who has decided to conclude his leap in a certain position and does it with the utmost self-confidence.

Even though Lars Kaj involuntarily started to brake, the car had so much momentum that they were approaching fast, and the helicopter was growing before their eyes so that it was soon just as large as it had been a moment earlier. It was no longer sealed and technologically unapproachable as before: the door of the cockpit opened, and two policemen appeared with their uniform jackets flapping and ran in opposite directions in order to block the road on both sides of the aircraft.

"Stop," shouted Niels, "stop, stop, stop!"

"It's too late!" yelled the Shadow. He was now completely hunched over the wheel, his glasses riding on the tip of his nose and his eyes popping out of their sockets as he stared forward at the insane obstacles that had suddenly been stacked in front of him. The policemen waved their arms and stretched them out to hold him back, but in a strange way they weren't convincing enough, and not as scary as the helicopter with the metallic voice either. Then Mik caught sight of a movement that was unmistakable. One of the policemen reached his hand down toward his belt and started to unsnap his holster!

"Watch out," yelled Mik, "watch out! He's going to shoot!"

It was too late to watch out for anything. Using the hood ornament as a gunsight, the Shadow aimed for something that looked like an opening — or would have to be an opening, if the policeman on the right didn't want to give his life for the sake of a car thief. A junkie who was a car thief!

Niels and Mik braced themselves. They didn't have any voice left, their throats were dry, and their tongues lay like a rough snail's foot pressed against their palates. They just had time to see the shadow of the helicopter's rotor circling on the cement around the lumpy outline of the aircraft, then the officer was life-sized, his eyes wide behind his glasses, his arms and legs stiff and spread-eagled like a jumping jack. Then he was gone, jumping aside to save his life, and the car zoomed past.

Their relief lasted only a moment.

"We have to get out of here," howled Lars Kaj. "Away from the freeway. It's our only chance."

Can't he just stop, thought Mik, just stop nice and quiet and pull over to the side. Wouldn't that be the best thing to do?

Then through the back window Mik looked at the helicopter, which had sealed itself up again. The officers were no longer on the roadway, and half a minute later it tilted upward and came after them again. Nobody had shot at them, but they hadn't given up the chase either. That was obvious enough. Without climbing very high the helicopter set a course straight for them. To Mik it looked for a moment as if it would land on the trunk or maybe grab the entire car between its two wheels and lift it up and fly away with the car and them too, like the giant Roc with its huge egg in its claws. The aircraft was right above them now, pacing the car like a shadow. The voice came again: "CS 62 881. Your irresponsibility is aggravating the circumstances. Is that understood?

CS 62 881, surrender at once. This is your last chance. CS 62 881, this is the police, the police . . ." The word reverberated.

Neither Mik nor Niels had any idea what was going to happen next. They still held on tight to their seats, yet sat resigned, staring to the left and right while the voice sputtered and blared, and the turbulence from the big propeller made the car rock. They also glanced at the Shadow, who had become one with the steering wheel and didn't even seem to be aware of what was going on around him.

"What if it lands again?" said Mik in a small voice.

Lars Kaj shook his head. Then he motioned up ahead, and Mik turned to look. Big white arrows curved from left to right across the concrete, and now blue road signs were whizzing by at shorter and shorter intervals — that's what it looked like, anyway — and before either Niels or Mik could say a word, Lars Kaj forced the car to the right and down the curving exit ramp at fifty miles an hour, even though it said 25 the whole way, and the left rear fender was hammered into the concrete three times, and the smell of burnt rubber from the screeching tires spread through the car. There was no need to let themselves be shot by the police, Mik thought for an instant; Lars Kaj was man enough to take care of all of them.

Then they were out on a straight road again, and even though it was only a third as wide as the concrete highway and twisted a lot more, the Shadow still managed to get the speed up, and because of the trees along the side of the road it seemed as though the helicopter was forced to fly a little higher than it had before. It wasn't sitting right over the roof anymore, but the pressure from the rotor blades was still noticeable, and they could hear the metallic voice now and then: "CS 62 881, CS 62 881!"

"What are we going to do?" hiccupped Niels. He was prone to attacks of the shakes, and now it looked as if he was shivering as he sat there hugging himself.

"We'll lose them sooner or later," said the Shadow, "but they've probably called for reinforcements. Maybe they put up a roadblock ahead. We've got to get out of here!"

"You keep on saying that!" Mik could hear that his voice was shaking.

"Have you got a better idea?"

The helicopter appeared low in front of them again, very low. It seemed to have decided that now was the time, now was the end game, now it was going to be finished, no matter what the cost.

The situation could hardly be worse, and Mik could see no way out of it. Either the police would catch them or they would die in a car crash. He was on the verge of resigning himself to the thought and maybe even wishing for the latter way out; when he looked out over the dashboard, the prospects were grim. Earlier he had thought they had been pursued the whole time because they had broken certain rules, and he could understand that this wasn't allowed, but he still didn't really understand the scope of the rules. It seemed unreasonable that the primitive break-in attempt at the laundromat would elicit the reactions he was now experiencing. On the other hand, their "crime" became bigger and more abominable with each new thing they did. They had stolen a car, that was undeniable, and they had not obeyed the police order to surrender. They had driven much too fast, yes, they had even tried to kill a police officer. If he hadn't jumped for his life, that would have been the end.

Mik held his hand in front of his face as he tried to concentrate. His thoughts did not come in a coherent series, they pounded down on him from left and right like angry birds and tugged at his conscience.

Here they were driving along in flight from something they hadn't wished on themselves, but which they were getting more and more involved in. At the same time they faced a sinister threat which wasn't explained either: the column of military vehicles, the flashing stars moving across the sky, the talk of war. What did it mean, and why were they the ones who were being forced into something that seemed like it would never end? It was as if the journey through the cave, yes, the whole idea of the cave, was being repeated here. They were coming closer and closer to a flaming exit that they ought to turn their backs on but were being irresistibly drawn toward. There had been a secret once, Mik recalled, a pleasant one he could have taken to bed with him and felt happy about before he went to sleep. Now there was no secret; it had changed into a reality that Mik in his wildest imagination would never have been able to dream up. But there was something recognizable about it all (and that was perhaps the most terrifying thing): he was, and really felt himself to be, part of it, and he was responsible for it. The thought was hard to bear, and that's why he also wished for the whole thing to be over.

Then he opened his eyes and saw that Niels was still sitting with his arms protectively around himself, and he saw the Shadow — with his ridiculous hat and his coat that was way too big and his thick glasses — with his arms hanging over the wheel, wildly intent on carrying out the escape. He realized that if he, if *they,* were ever to get a chance to go home, yes, to be saved, then it wouldn't do any good to give up, no matter what else happened.

"The belt," Lars Kaj said suddenly, "put the belt on!" He nodded in the direction of Mik's ear, but Mik didn't understand a thing.

"Put the belt on," yelled the Shadow, "yeah, you too!" He nodded back in Niels' direction.

"Seat belts, you airheads. Don't you think it's about time?"

Mik looked around and discovered that a wide belt was hanging next to him in the car.

"Yeah, that's it. Put it on!"

` They passed a bicycle with a motor on it, and the rider had to go halfway off the shoulder to avoid being sucked along with them.

"You moped idiot," screamed the Shadow, "move your ass!"

Mik managed to pull the belt down, and after fumbling a little he got it on and fastened the clasp so it locked. Niels was working on the same thing in the back seat.

Mik couldn't help smiling. There he sat — with his life in his hands, while the car was eating up the road — in a seat belt. His face grew serious again. He hoped the seat belt would help.

7

With the helicopter still in front of them at a low altitude, they were driving uphill. They could have strung a rope between the car and the aircraft; it seemed that they were being pulled along, the pilot was keeping the distance so precisely. But suddenly the car started to cough, and their speed dropped. The Shadow stomped hard on the accelerator but it didn't help, and Mik saw that the gas gauge was on empty.

They both shouted at once: "We're out of gas!"

Lars Kaj cursed and Mik saw that the helicopter had pulled a little ahead. It had not yet noticed that the car was losing speed.

"There *has* to be more in it," shouted the Shadow. "If we can just get over the hill, then the tank will be tipped the other way and we'll get another few drops out of it."

He shook the gearshift and new energy apparently shot into the engine; the car leaped forward. Then it slowed down.

The helicopter took a swing out over the field and was on its way back. Now it was aware of their predicament. Now it was aiming right at its prey. Even though it couldn't land on the road, but had to keep to the fields, they would be trapped if the car stopped. They neared the top of the hill, and with just one more lurch, cylinders banging and gears grinding, they made it over the top — and the gasoline flowed freely again.

It almost looked as though the helicopter was contracting, raising its wheels up underneath to become more compact, more streamlined, enraged that its prey once more seemed about to escape. The machine tilted with its rotor pointed forward and came at them in a dive that made them think for a moment that it was going to shave off the tops of the trees along the road with its propellers. Lars Kaj put the gas pedal to the floor — it was a short respite until the next hill started — and they felt again how the tons of metal hovering above them almost sat down on their roof and pressed them into the ground in a whirlwind. No one said a word, not even the loudspeakers from the helicopter. Now the game would be decided, and words were obviously superfluous.

For a moment Mik seriously thought that the pilot intended to crush them with his machine, even if it cost him his life, but they were still driving, they were driving at full speed and waiting for the hill, and they could already see the pavement sloping up ahead of them. The Shadow pressed his foot on the gas pedal with all his might, standing up in his seat, and without regard for the trees or the ditch or the impossible angle he turned the car off the pavement and down a wheel rut to the left. As they zoomed across the road they left a black, burning trail — the car would have flipped over if the Shadow hadn't braked as hard as he could for a second — but then they raced on, and he whooped like a cowboy: "We're losing them, we're losing them!"

But it wasn't like before. They didn't lose the helicopter; it pulled off an almost equally risky maneuver and was instantly on top of them again. Now they could feel no difference between the shaking from above and below. The downdraft beat against the roof, and underneath the car rocks and gravel shot up as though they were riding through a minefield with exploding mines under them. If Niels and Mik hadn't had seat belts on, they would have been thrown to the ceiling and maybe even out of the car. A door flew open, and it was impossible to close it. They held on tight, and Lars Kaj's knuckles were white on the steering wheel. None of them had noticed before, but when they came around a bend and a hubcap flew off and spun off crazily through the air, they saw the end of the road ahead.

It was a dead end, and right behind it towered a pine forest. The pines were tall, taller than those back home at the ruin. Mik just managed to register this before he saw that the road ended at a house, a shed with a flat roof, a garage. All at once the engine quit, but their momentum was so great that the car kept going at an insane speed, and Mik saw through his fingers how all three of them were sitting bent over with their hands on their faces, their eyes squeezed shut and their mouths closed. Then everything turned dark and light at the same time, wood splinters and glass whirled around their ears, and the sudden stop felt like an enormous kick in the stomach. The seat belts cut into their bodies but their guts wanted to keep going, their hearts were jammed into their throats, and their internal organs felt like they were being ripped apart. All three of them screamed, and when Mik blinked again he saw that the Shadow was slung halfway up the dashboard and that the steering column had snapped. The safety glass of the windshield shattered before them like a cloud of stars, and there was a moment of inexplicable total silence, and then it fell, the glass broken into bits, like a curtain coming down.

Through the smashed wall of the shed and the empty windshield they saw how the helicopter continued forward, as though it had actually been sitting on the roof of the car and was now flung off by a catapult. They couldn't believe their eyes, and even though they were dazed and almost unconscious they opened their eyes so wide it hurt; it was as if their eyes were screaming, for the helicopter couldn't manage to pull up. During the chase the pilot must have been concentrating so much on the fleeing car that he had forgotten the course, forgotten that there were obstacles, forgotten that a helicopter can do a lot but not everything, and now it was too late — even though the machine was still flying. They felt a heart-stopping nausea: the angle of inclination was much too steep, the heavy fuselage toppled slowly backward, as though the pilot wanted one last try at climbing up the vertical pine trees, then the aircraft tipped over completely, stood dancing uncertainly for a moment on top of its own propeller, and then plunged, with a raging cracking of splintered wood, like a gigantic electric razor into the trees. There was a moment's pause, again, and then the world expanded, a flame burst up — first as a small but concentrated bubble of light that dazzled them — then outward like an exhalation, a cough of heat and radiation that with its fiery power made the daytime look dark, there was so much light in it.

They raised their arms and tried to take cover from the firestorm. It was a purely physical storm, but inside themselves they felt an uproar too, which threatened to explode them like deep-sea fish that had inadvertently come ashore. What had happened? Why were they here, and what had they done? None of the questions or feelings were clearly defined, they just welled up like an irresistible pressure in the midst of the struggle to get out, to escape, to save their lives. Rivulets of burning gasoline ran down the slope toward them. Maybe there was a danger of more explosions; they would have to go the other way. What about the men in the machine? There had been people in the helicopter, they had seen them themselves. They had seen them on the road and inside the glass cockpit, they had heard the voice: "CS 62 881, CS 62 881!" Now there were no more voices and nothing moved, there was only a loud, continuous roar from the gasoline bonfire, which little by little took on a broader undertone as the fire spread to the pine trees.

Niels and Mik were already standing in the splintered garage when they noticed that one of the Shadow's arms was hanging funny. He had only gotten halfway down off the dashboard, and Mik ran back to help him. He wanted to grab hold of Lars Kaj and pull him out, but the strange angle of his arm hanging over the wheel made him hesitate. A layer of dust covered Lars Kaj's glasses, and his hat had rolled off. He might have been blind. For a moment Mik thought that maybe he was, but the arm . . . what was he going to do with that arm? And what if he couldn't see either? There were so many decisions to make that he was paralyzed. He felt weighed down by the events, and everything he had experienced, everything that had fallen on him like an avalanche, whirled around in his head. What should you do in the midst of a catastrophe, what should you do when you had no idea what to do?

The temptation to give up was great. It would be a relief just to fall down and start crying. He wasn't so old that he had forgotten about crying — the way it's suddenly there and can't be held back, crying as a weapon and as protection, the sweetness of crying when you just let it go. Right in front of his nose lay the Shadow, and his strange arm was like a plea: Do something, help me, don't just stand there! A broken arm is terrible, but it can be set, they can always find the correct angle even though the whole thing looks crooked, just get moving!

He saw Lars Kaj blink behind his dusty, soot-blackened glasses. He could see that he was moving his eyes like someone who could see. Mik got hold of him and dragged him carefully out of the front seat. The Shadow found the ground with his feet, and even though his arm was dangling, he started to walk, with his other arm around Mik's shoulder. Niels was beside them, and they hopped and stumbled forward away from the fire and the crushed garage shed. Just as they passed the driveway, Niels saw that an egg had rolled out of a little bunch of straw and twigs in the corner of the garage. He hesitated involuntarily, and although the fire behind them felt like a gas oven turned up high, he stopped and held the others back, bending down to grab the egg and two others hidden in the corner.

"Eggs," he said like a madman, "eggs, eggs, eggs."

Maybe he really had gone crazy. There was no time to think about it; they limped and danced onward, past the house, which lay deserted with its windows closed and curtains drawn. Only a white hen walked around alone in the yard, stopping to stare at them as though she didn't understand much about what had happened but was still sure that they were the ones who had stolen her eggs.

They kept on limping and dancing at a wobbling, awkward pace for a ways down the road, then they turned into the woods again. They didn't think about the direction, they just had to get as far away from the sound of the burning helicopter as possible. At first it sounded like a constant booming and wheezing, as if someone was banging on big barrels and blowing into them at the same time, but after a while the sound ebbed away and turned into a crackling that finally vanished altogether. They must be upwind of it. In the part of the forest where they were now, it smelled of moss and leaves; only their own clothes, ripped and filthy, retained the bitter smell of smoke and oil. Out of breath, they leaned up against a beech tree that towered far above the other trees and seemed to disappear in the sky. With his back to the tree the Shadow slowly slid down and sat on the ground. He was pale; his face was almost the same color as the gray bark of the tree.

"Damn it to hell," he said, "my arm makes me want to puke." He shook his head. "What a load of crap."

They couldn't tell if he meant his arm — or everything.

Mik squatted down. "Shouldn't we bandage it up?" he asked.

The Shadow glowered at the awkward-looking limb. "We've got to get going," he said.

Mik wanted to protest, but Lars Kaj kept talking.

"We've got to keep moving. We have to get to the city. It's our only hope."

"You keep saying that!"

"Because it's true." He wiped his good arm across his glasses. "You can't disappear here. Not even in a forest. You saw for yourselves, damn it. Didn't you? Haven't you seen enough?" His voice was shrill. "Anyway, I can't stand it anymore . . ." His voice broke. "I can't, I just can't."

His mouth contorted and he started to sob. Mik pulled back a little in shock. The Shadow was suddenly different. He was crying!

"I've got to have a fix," he mumbled. "That's the only thing," he looked at Mik, "the only thing that matters. All the rest is a pile of shit. It's nothing but shit, can't you see that?"

Again he wiped his face with his good arm, and tears and oil mixed with the soot so that all the contours were smeared.

"Fucking arm!" he said in a rage, staring down at it. His glasses were partly clean, and the gleam in his eye that Mik had noticed earlier seemed to have returned.

Lars Kaj stared at Mik. His voice was calmer now. "Only the city can take care of it. In the city you can disappear, in the city you can escape. That's where your friends are. Everywhere else they treat you like shit. Don't you think I know it? I've tried it — and now what?"

He wanted to strike out with his bad arm, but the pain shot through it and rushed up like a pallor into his face. "Ow, damn it." He raised his head again. "Give me one of those eggs."

Shadows undulated across Niels' face. His hair was blackened, and his curls looked like snakes. He leaned forward and stuck a hand into his windbreaker. When it emerged there was an egg in it.

"OK," said the Shadow, "we'll eat an egg. And then we take off. It can't be more than twenty kilometers farther."

He took the egg, and Niels gave Mik one and kept one for himself.

"I don't know this area, but if we keep walking and stay away from the roads and hide whenever we come close to any people, we should make it, if they don't go totally berserk — after what happened." He dropped his head.

"But it wasn't our fault," he yelled suddenly, "it wasn't just *our* fault!"

Again he wanted to shake his fist, but the pain in his bad arm stopped him, and his face contorted. "Oh fuck it all," he said, "it probably doesn't matter anyway, nothing matters. They always win in the end."

Mik didn't know what he should do. He sat with his egg in his hand, gazing for a moment at its strange, beautiful shape. He couldn't intervene, he didn't know what he should say to Lars Kaj or how he could help. He also hadn't understood what his friend meant by "a fix" or something like that. There were gaps again, they kept coming up all the time. When the Shadow talked about the city, Mik understood that it all made sense to *him*. But Mik would have preferred to hide in the woods — or would he? Didn't he feel more secure in the city too, where he came from? Wasn't he less afraid there than when he stood in front of the summer house and stared at the black vault of the sky or crept into the cave he had found in the ruins?

The egg in his hand had a soothing effect. He carefully ran his fingers over the smooth shell. Hens pecked corn and laid eggs. It was simple and straightforward. What people were doing was a little harder to figure out. With the egg in his hand he felt for the first time in several days something un-broken — that there was a connection, a continuation, a line. Then he caught sight of Lars Kaj, who sat helpless with his egg in his hand and didn't know how he was going to get it open and eat it without dropping it. Mik carefully put down his own egg and crept on all fours over to the Shadow.

"Let me help you," he said.

He took the egg from the Shadow and noticed that his hands were shaking. If you dropped an egg, it broke. If you got lost in a forest, you might never get home. If you did what you weren't supposed to, then what? Mik looked for his knife, remembered that he must have lost it a long ways back, and if one of the men in black or the police hadn't found it by now, it was probably lying between the grass embankment and the back wall of the laundromat. Then he put his finger-nail against the side of the egg near the top and pressed. It made a hole. With another finger he managed to pry off the top a little. Lars Kaj took the egg in his good hand and swallowed the contents in two big gulps. Mik and Niels watched him. In a funny way it seemed that he always knew what he was doing.

Mik crept back and found his own egg. Hunger, which had been pushed aside before, replaced the queasiness he had felt for a moment when Lars Kaj swallowed the yolk and the white raw. He could swallow the egg whole if he had to! Again his hands shook so much he was about to drop the egg, but it wasn't nervousness, it was hunger. He got the top pried off and put the egg to his mouth, he sucked and slobbered and felt how the fluid yet elastic substance slipped down his throat. He also felt how neglected his insides were, how they accepted it, and for a moment he saw the image of the red oatmeal package with the boy on it and the shining sun. There were things he missed. There were big things he had lost, maybe even the biggest things of all. He took a deep breath. How peaceful his world had been, how secure his life.

The beech tree towered up between them, and sound and motion came from the treetop. It felt like sitting next to a mast, but none of them had any idea which direction the ship was sailing, whether they were lost or saved. The city was the only goal, but was there any plan? Lars Kaj's awful arm seemed to point in all directions at once. There was no doubt that it ought to be bandaged up. Mik stared at Niels. He had been a boy scout, after all, maybe he knew how.

"You have to get that arm bandaged up," Mik said forcefully.

"I'm not going to have anything bandaged up." The Shadow shook his head; he was still quite pale.

"Niels," said Mik, "can't you . . . haven't you tried this?"

"Sure," he said quietly, "I learned how, but I never tried it before." The egg was gone, and his eyes looked a little more normal. "But we don't have any bandage."

Mik squatted down. "How about a shirt, can't you use that?"

"Well, maybe."

"I don't want any bandage on," snapped the Shadow.

The others paid no attention to him. Mik slipped out of his windbreaker and pulled off his shirt and undershirt. Together they tore the cloth, and when they folded the shirt they actually got it to look like a bandage. It was primitive, but it would work.

Mik knelt in front of the Shadow. "Can you move your arm?"

Lars Kaj shook his head.

"May I . . . ?"

It was almost as if the broken arm were another creature or a bodily part that didn't belong to the Shadow. Even he stared at it like a foreign thing.

"Careful," he said, "but make it quick."

Niels and Mik moved in close to him and put a sling around his neck. Mik hesitated a moment, then he took hold of the crushed arm that was dangling there and moved it into a position that seemed more natural. There was a moment's pause while they slipped it into the sling, and then Lars Kaj let out a scream that made them pull back in fright. His face seemed to melt for a moment — the furrows smoothed out, his glasses became a prop, his crazy hair something glued on, and all that was left was a baby's amazement that something can be so unexpected and hurt so incredibly much.

When the scream stopped, all three of them lay shaken. A hole had been ripped into a place in their consciousness where defenses could no longer be mobilized. Something hurt so much that you couldn't defend yourself against it, certain events were so catastrophic and overwhelming that there was almost no defense at all. Red and green bands of light passed through Mik's consciousness; he felt himself lifted and flung higher up in space than he had ever been before, and it was impossible to say whether he would ever land on his feet again. Now the Shadow's arm was in the sling, at least, and he wasn't screaming anymore. Could he be dead?

Mik opened his eyes and saw that his friend had leaned his head against the tree trunk and sat there panting.

"I'd rather go cold turkey," he said after a while.

"What?"

Niels looked as though he had suddenly been awakened from a trance too.

"When you've been tripping for a long time, and then they start taking the stuff away from you, goddamn it, or it's impossible to get hold of a fix ... No, I don't know. Maybe I'd still rather break an arm."

The Shadow was talking in riddles. The magic word "fix" had been mentioned again.

"Fix?" asked Mik.

Lars Kaj closed his eyes in exhaustion.

"A fix, yeah," he mumbled, "a tiny little fix, a little white powder, kiddo, that you cook a while and then jab into your arm, and then whoosh — you're in heaven!"

He opened his eyes and stared at Mik with a twisted grin. "And then everything's gone! Then you can fly, and sleep, and do both at the same time. Then things stop being crazy, like now. And everything makes sense, and it's all beautiful and simple, not ..."

He flung out his good arm in a deprecating gesture. "Bleaahh . . ."

A little later he leaned forward and tried to get to his feet, without success. He groaned.

"We have to get going, you hear me? We can't sit here playing therapy group."

The paleness in his face was accentuated by the color of his hair. He was a painted doll sitting across from them, not a human being. But they still knew it was Lars Kaj.

"What are we going to do?" asked Mik a while later.

"I told you already. We have to get to Copenhagen. I've got friends there. They can help us."

"Your father and mother?" Niels asked cautiously.

"Aw, for — " Lars Kaj turned his head away. "I've never seen my father, and my mother? Sure, she's nice enough, but mixed up. And she's sick to death of me. But there are other people." He sounded hopeful, but rather guarded.

None of them had dared mention what had happened to the helicopter.

"They'll have to help us out." The Shadow's glasses flashed. "Because the others will eat us alive!"

The Shadow pulled his legs in under him and managed to get to his feet with great exertion. There was always something quite elegant and grown-up about the way he spoke, even though he just looked like a little kid playing trick or treat. He seemed seasoned, as if he had lived at least twice as long as the other two. Had he gotten any smarter? Mik couldn't tell. For the time being he was dependent on him, and he had no doubt about the fact that he liked Lars Kaj.

Niels got up too, and they stood in a triangle looking at

each other. In the woods they were outlaws. Wouldn't they be in the city too?

"That actually helped," Lars Kaj said, looking down at his broken arm. Then he looked at Niels. "And it was a good thing you went berserk and started acting goofy in that garage. Thanks for the egg. I never would have thought I'd have a broody hen for a friend."

With his good hand he pressed his hat down on his head; he turned around and started walking. A moment later the others followed.

They trudged for a long time through the woods, but several times they passed close to roads both large and small, where the sound of traffic grew to a roar. Among stiles and woodpiles they crept through high grass out to a point where they had a good view, and they saw that cars were moving in close ranks, apparently on their way out of the city. There was also a lot of military traffic, yet the number of passenger cars was more striking. Mik and Niels had never seen so many cars in their entire lives, but the most remarkable thing was the baggage piled on their roofs and sticking out the windows, where table legs and tent poles were crammed in between all the people stuffed into the seats.

Lars Kaj turned his head toward them. "Something's up," he whispered. "There's something wrong . . ."

His voice was drowned out by a flock of the awkward triangles, which flew low over the road with engines shrieking. Mik pressed his face to the grass and held his ears.

"What's that?" His voice was strained, as if the sound waves were trying to shove it back down his throat.

"Jet fighters. I don't know whose. They went by too fast."

"Where are they going?" Niels had his face almost buried in the grass.

"Who?"

"The people."

"I don't know. They're leaving. It looks like they just want to get away. You don't take off for your summer house *that* way."

Even Lars Kaj's voice sounded uncertain. For the first time it seemed as though he wasn't sure what was happening either.

"We've got to talk to somebody," he said.

"Talk to somebody? But . . ."

"They're looking for three of us, right?" Lars Kaj's voice was in charge again. "One of us will go down somewhere and ask what's happening. This isn't normal. It doesn't look like a regular Sunday outing. And we can't just go to Copenhagen without knowing anything. Maybe it's our big chance!"

Mik didn't understand what he meant. Why couldn't they just hide and keep on running together until they reached their goal? If there was a goal. What was it they had to know, and why did the Shadow all at once seem so excited again?

"But maybe you're too scared," Lars Kaj said suddenly. "You're probably just a couple of chickenshits after all." His eyes moved restlessly behind his glasses.

"Never mind, I can do it myself." He started to get up, but Mik got hold of the tail of his long jacket and pulled him down. Maybe he was a little too rough, because the Shadow howled when he toppled over and rolled halfway over his broken arm.

"I'm sorry," Mik whispered, "I'm sorry."

In the silence that followed they could hear the sound of

the cars. It was an uninterrupted stream, yet the noise had something subdued and hesitant about it. The speed must be slower than it had been on the big highway the day before; the military column also looked much more cautious and less aggressive than it would have at a higher speed. The vehicles seemed weighed down by burdens, perhaps with something more than what was visible with the naked eye. The sheer number of them brought the speed down.

In his mind's eye Mik saw another scene from the day before: the women in the bakery who had bought not one but six loaves of bread, not one pound of butter but twelve. Was there really talk of hoarding? Did the column of cars on its way out of town mean that it was an evacuation? Mik had been "evacuated" himself from town for a little while, because "anything might happen." Nothing ever did happen, and he had a funny feeling that he was the only one in the whole city who had to suffer the humiliation of being separated from his parents and his sister for that reason.

What he was witnessing now looked different, more serious. He didn't completely understand what the Shadow meant, that it might be their big chance. Maybe he meant that the police had better things to do than go looking for them, if an entire city was being evacuated. He would have to find out. He also partly understood why Lars Kaj felt the same way.

"I'll go down there," Mik said.

"Down where?"

Mik didn't feel so sure. "Down there. To the road," he said.

"What do you want to go down to the road for? You

think they're going to stop? And don't you think there'll be cops all over the place?" Lars Kaj was lying on his side. "We'll sneak farther through the woods, and if we come to a house, then you can go down and ask for water or something. And maybe find out what's happening. And make sure to take off if they start anything!" He touched Mik's shoulder. "We'll have to do something about the way you look, though. You can't be seen like that."

Mik had forgotten about how he looked. When he looked at the others, he could imagine that his appearance might not be quite normal. To top it off, he had used his shirt for the Shadow's bandage. He must look terrible. For a moment he thought of what his mother would have said if he showed up looking like this, then he pushed the thought aside. Maybe Niels could spy instead of him? He looked less miserable — at least his clothes did.

"What about Niels?"

"What about him?"

"Wouldn't it be better if *he* went to find out?"

The Shadow looked at him. "Yeah, he can if he wants to."

Soot had settled in the wrinkles in Niels' face. That is, he didn't have any real wrinkles, but when he squinted out of nervousness or because of the bright sunlight, he scrunched up the skin of his face, and when he relaxed, all the dirt was left behind in stripes. Now the lines moved.

"Why do I have to?" he asked.

"Nobody says you have to. Nobody says that anybody has to do anything. We can just lay around here."

"Then let's go back — to the place where we came from."

"To the town? You've got to be kidding. That would be

like running right into their arms. Didn't you understand that I *have* to get to Copenhagen? I don't *feel* like dealing with that other shit anymore."

Niels looked away. "We've got to go back."

"Yeah, you probably do." The Shadow lay on his back with his face in the sunshine. "By the way, you never told me where you came from. Is it a secret?"

Niels shrugged. His expression changed, and he looked unhappy.

"We . . . can't really explain it," said Mik.

For some reason he felt as if he let the Shadow down. But how were they supposed to tell him where they came from? It was impossible, he would never believe it, and who knew if it was true?

The Shadow chuckled to himself. "You'd think you came up out of a hole in the ground."

Niels sat up straight as if he had gotten a shock. "We did," he shouted, "we came up out of a hole in the ground!"

"Sure, sure," said the Shadow, "take it easy." He turned his face toward Niels. "I don't give a shit. As far as I'm concerned you could have come out of a hole in somebody's ass. Right now that's not the problem. If you want to keep secrets, I won't stick my nose into it. I come from a hole too, you better believe it." He got an almost wistful smile at the thought. "And I never should have left."

The slow sound from the road boomed up toward them.

"Now I want to go down there too." Lars Kaj slowly raised himself to his knees. He looked all around and then nodded, and they started to creep back the same direction they had come.

After a while they got up and starting walking. It was obvious that every step was costing the Shadow more pain, but he just plowed on and didn't stop until they spotted something white and black, which didn't look like trees, shining up ahead. Then he made a sign to the others, and they huddled together in a little triangle and squatted down.

"It's a house," whispered the Shadow. "It looks like a forest ranger's house, or whatever they're called. I'll go down there myself."

Niels and Mik stiffened. Then they stretched out their hands in protest and shook their heads.

The Shadow pushed his hat back on his head. He laughed. "OK, we'll send Niels down. He looks the nicest. Wipe off his face a little first."

Mik fished out his handkerchief, knelt in front of his friend, and started rubbing at the black stuff on his face. It was on there good. Then he remembered his mother — he raised the cloth to his mouth and spit on it. Niels didn't budge an inch, but sat there patiently as Mik removed the worst patches of soot and oil from his face.

"Ask if you can have a little drink of water. They have no right to deny you that. And then see if you can find out what happened — what *is* happening, that is — and approximately where we are."

Niels nodded. It was clear that he had made a decision and was now going to follow it. Mik touched his shoulder as a sign that he was ready; then Niels stood up and walked straight ahead through the branches and down toward the house. Mik felt a pang. It was the first time they hadn't been near each other for hours. The Shadow sat calmly beside him.

It was obvious that he was used to waiting, used to strange situations in which you just had to control yourself — or go crazy. Mik felt a quiver inside. He would have to say something if he was going to stand the tension. He looked at the Shadow.

"Does it hurt?"

The Shadow nodded.

"Don't you think you ought to see a doctor?"

"Sure. But it has to wait."

"What if it starts healing crooked?"

"Then we'll break it open again. Or the sawbones will. It happens all the time."

"Yeah, but what if it gets worse?"

"Everything gets worse."

Mik huddled into himself. It was a warm day, but he was still aware that he didn't have a shirt on. They were inside the woods, and the shadows were deep. He had also been sweating earlier, when they were walking and walking. Now he was a little cold. He knew what his mother would have said: "If you perspire you should change your underclothes." His father always did. Just mowing the lawn or riding his bike uphill for too long would make him break out in a sweat. Then he would change his undershirt. But here there was nothing to change into.

"We found this cave," he said nonchalantly, more to himself than to anyone else. "We went into it . . ."

It was impossible to tell whether Lars Kaj was listening or not. He was sitting Indian-style next to Mik, his arm in a sling, and his eyes were half closed behind his glasses.

"I was the one who found the cave — "

Mik didn't get any farther before a sound broke in that seemed all too familiar and yet terribly startling. They should have known, they should have thought of that! It was a dog barking — and not only barking, it sounded like it was coming closer too, and when they jumped up they saw that Niels was on his way back with a big gray shadow jumping up and down at him, a German shepherd the size of a wolf.

Lars Kaj swore between his teeth. The sudden movement had made his arm dangle in the sling. He gasped, but the impending troubles pushed the physical pain and the more long-range anxiety into the background — especially when they saw that the dog had bitten hold of Niels' arm and was flaying what was left of his windbreaker to shreds, while he screamed and the dog frothed at the mouth.

Now this wasn't the first dog they'd been attacked by in their lives, and even though it was bigger and more terrifying than any dog Mik had ever seen, it was obvious that their experiences and the challenges they faced and the desperate situation made them act both more decisively and more tactically. Niels had enough to do coping with his fear and the continuing attacks from the slavering, snarling dog, and there was a moment when Mik felt like following his impulse to run, run, run. He couldn't run away from Niels, especially not now, and when he saw the Shadow moving in a circle at top speed in back of the dog, all the while striking at it and yelling at the top of his lungs, he started to do the same. There was no doubt that the sight of the two new attackers and their movements confused the dog and made it even more enraged and bewildered, so it started biting and jumping every which way. Then Niels slipped free for a moment, and when he had collected himself and discovered that he wasn't the only one the animal was attacking, he threw himself into the dance. They were like three Indians circling around a bonfire or a sacrificial animal that was becoming more and more aware of its own fate, because it had to hold its own against the mounting savagery and wildness of the boys. The dog was unable to figure out where the enemy was. Every time it leapt out it got a kick from the other side, and every time it snapped there was a new movement to defend itself against and attack.

The circle kept on turning around its untamable center, moving down toward the house at the same time. Near an excavation to the right of the entrance lay a pile of broken bricks and rocks — it seemed that someone was in the process of building an air-raid shelter or bunker on the lot and had given up the job in the middle of it. While the three of them kept on teasing and baiting the dog, fending off its attacks all the while, they had time to bend down during the dance and pick up rocks, which they threw at the dog, while their ferocity seemed to increase in power. The dog yelped when it was hit, its rage grew, and in a kind of terrible reciprocation the bounds of reason in the fight were shattered. It was as if all dogs were contained in this single one, as if all the terrifying dogs that jump at you behind fences, pop up from under hedges, born as the shadows of the dark with glowing maws in the world of every child, had merged in this one spiky-haired, gray-striped, urine-colored monster. It was as if all their fear of the unknown and the instinctually uncontrollable found its way up to the surface and sought revenge every time a rock left their hands and with a crack or a hollow thud struck the dog's head or body. What before had only resembled a ritual now turned into a real one, for it was a matter of exorcism. It was not only the dog, it was the accumulated fright itself they were fighting, and there was no thought of stopping before the sacrifice was annihilated.

As the dog gradually became more and more exhausted and its movements grew slower and slower, they had time to pick up larger, heavier lumps of stone. They lifted the rocks over their heads and heaved them at the animal with their mouths open and their eyes wide. Finally one of the stones hit the dog above the eye, there was a crack, and it fell to its knees howling, trying to cover its eye with one paw, or shove what was now flowing out of it back in. It was a quite helpless, awkward movement, like a cripple trying to walk with a cane that's much too short.

"Kill it," howled Niels, "kill it!" There was a mixture of madness and profound fright in his voice.

Niels stood with a piece of brick raised above his head; maybe it was himself he was calling to, for in the next instant he hurled the stone with all his might onto the head of the crawling German shepherd, which fell over in the gravel and stretched out its paws in supplication as it slowly opened its mouth wide, as though wanting to say something important very distinctly. It didn't make a sound.

Everything was quiet. The three boys stood frozen in positions like ballet dancers; then they dropped their arms, the Shadow supporting his broken arm with the other, Niels turning halfway around and stumbling over to a bush, where he bent over and threw up. It was the only thing they could hear now, this suppressed, explosive sound that turned into a retching, a little half-choked cough, when there is nothing to throw up but raw egg and pure gall.

Mik kept staring at the dog. It was also frozen in its own development, and now seemed inquisitive, almost innocent. As if it really were surprised. Actually the dog had only done what it had been trained to do, and what instinct commanded, without ever thinking of the risk. This time it had been surprised; something had happened it hadn't counted on. So that happened to dogs too. For the moment Mik didn't connect himself with the dog's death. Sure, he had been involved in killing it, but only half consciously. First it had been a matter of self-defense, then it turned into something else; he didn't really know what it was. Something he couldn't resist, and which was sort of like . . . the dog's instinct? He had done what he thought was necessary, without thinking about it — and then a little bit more.

Mik blinked; it was true that things changed. Now they were really changing — he felt something stirring inside himself that he couldn't describe at all. He was tired but still excited. He felt sick to his stomach but wanted to sing. The sight of the dog shocked him, the whole nasty and awkward ceremony of death: the open mouth, the burst, smashed eyes — but at the same time he felt liberated. He had won, hadn't he? Wasn't he walking on, free and alive, while the enemy lay crushed, treading stiffly in its own slime and blood? He discovered that for several minutes he hadn't given a thought to his father or mother or sister. The "other world" had been forgotten. Was that what it took to be able to wipe out or forget your past, everything you were connected to, everything that determined your life? Did you have to kill a big gray dog in a strange forest?

Mik didn't know anything; the brief respite that action had given him was over now, and the thought of what his mother would say, if she saw what he had been involved in and was doing minute by minute, loomed up before him like a mountain. The possibility that someday, many years from now, maybe when she was dead, he would get mixed up in something, do something that she might not approve of, had crossed his mind a few times. But that inside of forty-eight hours he had . . . no, it was impossible to deal with, it was so impossible that it simply couldn't be true.

They stood stock still until they realized how quiet it actually was. The traffic down on the road was only faintly audible, and nobody came out of the house. If anyone had been inside, they would have come out during the fight with the dog because of the noise. There was no one around. The house just stood there, watching them blindly with its black windowpanes. Maybe the people who lived there were dead.

Niels wiped his mouth with his sleeve and came over to them. He walked in a big arc around the dog. Flies dozed among the hollyhocks; a bee took wing again and again, to hover a moment and then dip down. It was the 28th of July, 1988.

The Shadow limped over toward the house. He went up the three steps to the door and put his hand on the doorknob. Then he pushed against the door. It wasn't locked; they could walk right in. The stillness muttered around them, and no matter how terrifying the dog's rage had seemed before, this guarded, oppressive silence was just as frightening. Slowly they followed Lars Kaj into the house, where everything looked as though the residents had left in a hurry. The chairs were pushed back from the table as though people had just stood up, a boot lay leaning against the wall, children's toys were strewn across the steps, and the window shade was only open halfway. The chaos and confusion gave the impression of shock, because it was now all tangible and frozen in space like a viscous fluid they could almost lean against.

Then they heard a voice, and Lars Kaj turned to them with one finger raised. So somebody was home after all.

After they had stood there for a moment, and the voice kept on talking at the same level and seemed to be repeating the same message, they realized that it must be a radio. Mik felt a slight sense of security unfold. Maybe the bulletin would be on the radio after all.

The radio was in the kitchen. Even though it was speaking Danish, Mik and Niels had a hard time understanding what it was saying. The radio sat right beside the cutting board, where there lay a knife with a serrated edge and a partly sliced loaf of French bread. A crock of butter stood a little farther down the table.

The announcer kept repeating position readings of radio-active clouds and the possibility of radioactive fallout, strontium radiation, gamma radiation, and wind direction and speed. It sounded like a combination of weather report, coast guard report, and stock market quotations. They saw that the Shadow was shaking his head.

"What's the matter?" asked Niels.

"It's a pile of shit."

"Yeah, but *what's* a pile of shit? What does it mean?"

"They've evidently fired off some of their shit. Nuclear missiles, how do I know?" He listened again. "Maybe there'll be some news. That was an emergency broadcast, a warning."

"Is that why people are running away?" Mik had seen people running away from the highway in a German newsreel. That must be what was happening now.

"What's he saying?" Niels asked.

"I don't know." The Shadow sounded irritated. "I don't know any more than you do. It's been building up for a long time, for several years, and now it's finally happened."

"What?" yelled Niels.

"War with the Russians."

"The Russians?"

"Yeah, or the Americans, I don't know, I don't know shit. I only know that we have to get into town before the whole mess is blown to smithereens. I *have* to get back."

"But what about the others? They're running in the opposite direction!"

"I don't know what the others are doing, and I don't care. I can't desert my friends, and *they're* not running anywhere, I'll promise you that!"

A new voice came on the radio. Lars Kaj leaned forward to hear better. The reports were unconfirmed, said the voice, which sounded uncertain, pinched, and tense itself. It seemed probable that tactical nuclear weapons had been used on Genoa, Düsseldorf, Bristol, Liverpool, Rouen, Bilbao, Lisbon, and Hamburg . . .

They looked at each other. They knew that Hamburg, at

least, wasn't that far away. What kind of bombs were they? What was happening? They felt like their heads were going to explode because they couldn't find out anything!

The voice continued its list of other cities — also with Russian names. Then the first announcer returned and described the regulations that applied to the population of the greater Copenhagen region. Not only was highly concentrated fallout expected in the area, there was also a growing probability that Copenhagen had been targeted for a direct nuclear attack.

Mik heard the word "nuclear" like a violent opening and closing of his ears at once. Nuclear, nuclear, nuclear! He had heard the word before, but he felt that if he didn't find out what it meant — and it *had* to mean something horrible — he would go crazy. Out in the yard there lay a dead dog. Here — in front of the radio in a strange family's kitchen, he didn't know where — everything seemed much worse. He couldn't stand the fear and the uncertainty anymore. He had to find out *something*.

Mik moved close to the Shadow, facing him. "You're going to have to tell us what's going on," he said in a low voice. "We can't understand it. You have to help us."

Lars Kaj shook his head. His thick glasses were completely covered with sweat and dust and soot.

"I told you I don't know anything. But what they're shooting off ... they're atomic bombs. But you probably haven't heard of those either, huh?" He gestured helplessly with his good hand. "They must have been around forever. At least I feel like they've been around forever, but I think

they were invented at the end of World War II. Hiroshima —
haven't you heard of Hiroshima? Or Nagasaki? No, you
haven't heard of anything, don't tell me. It's hopeless."

"Tell us!" Mik's voice was threatening, and a little of the
wildness from before blinded him for a moment.

"They invented this bomb, by splitting atoms, I have no
idea how, but it was big, big as hell, and then they killed
100,000 people at once with it — "

"A hundred thousand!"

"Yeah, or 200,000 or 300,000, I don't know how many.
And now there are enough bombs to blow up the whole
world as many times as there were people blown up before,
and that's also the reason why we're not going to stand here
blabbering any longer. I don't want to, there isn't time, can't
you feel it? We've got to hurry, goddamn it, we've got to
hurry, it's the last minute, and I'm leaving *now*."

He turned on his heel and disappeared out the door.

For a moment Niels and Mik stood as if paralyzed; then
they looked at each other and ran after the Shadow. Neither
of them had any idea where they were or what to do. They
couldn't do anything without Lars Kaj. He was small and
funny-looking and spoke a language they barely understood
sometimes; but for quite obvious reasons, even though they
had seemed totally accidental from the beginning, they were
bound to him now. He had helped them — and had gotten
wounded! They also had a responsibility, although it was
impossible to predict the consequences of going with him to
Copenhagen. When all the rest of the people were apparently
going the opposite direction, that was the only solution.
Naturally they couldn't sit down next to the radio and wait

for a bulletin which they already could feel was never going to come. Without the Shadow they were totally alone in the world.

Even the minute when they stood in the empty, dead kitchen with the grating voice seemed like a foretaste of eternity. Every feeling of reality seemed to dissolve; stiffened ghosts, transparent figures, cracked voices filled the room — and still it was empty. There was no movement, no signals from anywhere, other than these specters and echoes of something dead and hopeless. The knife beside the bread on the cutting board cried out mutely; only the voice from the radio emitted its incomprehensible warnings and droned on about catastrophes whose scope and nature they had no chance of understanding. There was only one choice: after Lars Kaj!

Together they ran through the door, and together they passed the dog's cadaver, which seemed to call out to them for a long time with its open mouth, where the flies were already swarming convulsively. They saw the Shadow a little ways ahead, limping in his tattered coat, and it wasn't hard to catch up with him.

"What are we doing?" asked Mik.

"Why don't you two get lost?" Lars Kaj kept walking. He had a stubborn look on his face.

"Where do you want us to go?"

"Back where you came from."

"Yeah, but you don't understand."

"No, I don't understand shit."

Mik and Niels tried to keep up with him. "I'd like to explain . . ."

"There's nothing to explain. I understand all right. But it

would be crazy if you came with me to the city. I just have
to . . ."

"Yeah, but what are you going to do?"

"Get a fix."

"What's that?"

"I've got to have a fix — even if it's the last one in my
whole life. And visit a friend. He's a pusher."

Mik had heard about drug addicts. But how could Lars
Kaj be a drug addict? Drug addicts were *grownups*.

"Are you . . . are you a drug addict?"

The Shadow laughed wholeheartedly for the first time.
"You can bet your sweet ass I am. Four stars. Why did you
think I'd been at the detox center?"

Pieces started to fall into place, and a pattern emerged.
Mik couldn't envision what his new understanding involved;
on the contrary, he felt his uncertainty grow.

"But why?"

"Why what?"

"Why are you a drug addict? Are you sick?"

"Sick? I'm not the one who's fucking sick, man. Look
around! Didn't you hear what the guy on the radio said? It's
the end of the world. That's all there is to it. And it's been
going on for years." He turned to face Mik. "Now the shit
has hit the fan, and I intend to go out in style." He shook his
head. "I don't have the nerve for anything else. Anyway, my
arm hurts like hell."

Niels touched Mik on the shoulder. "Did he say that
Copenhagen is going to be bombed?"

"Possibly."

"Well, then what?"

"Poof," said Lars Kaj, "poof, bang, groink, it's all over."

"But they can't do that. They can't do that!"

"I'd say they can't help it. Why the hell should Copen-hagen be spared when all the rest of it is blown sky-high? It would be *so* lonesome." His cynicism was clear enough, but somewhere in his voice there was a sound vibrating that they couldn't quite figure out.

They had long since emerged from the woods and were walking through a suburban residential neighborhood. Everywhere the houses seemed empty and deserted; now and then a car would drive by rapidly and disappear toward the north. The thought that anyone might stop the boys and interrogate them seemed ludicrous. No one paid any atten-tion to them. It was as if they could go anywhere they liked and do anything they wanted to. Probably nobody would have stopped them if they decided to walk into one of the big houses. Maybe there was even food inside and something to drink — they didn't even think of it. They just trudged along, and when they passed an elderly man who stood by his garden gate looking angry, they stayed on the sidewalk and didn't cross to the other side.

"Scum," the man shouted suddenly after they had passed. "Scum and filth!"

The words echoed between the houses and were drowned out when a propellerless airplane zoomed over the area at treetop level. Mik noticed its shadow. He remembered that from home, from the summer house, but there it was slower, everything was slower.

It was almost impossible to imagine what his mother and father were doing right now. If they even existed! He repressed the thought quickly; it didn't help much to visualize Mr. and Mrs. Paslund as they sat at the little table out on the terrace in front of the house, trying to drink tea while they wondered what could have happened to Mik and Niels. How unhappy they must be. Were the people here happier? Was he? If his mother and father were alive, if they were living, even though they had to be without him if he never came back, then that was a great sorrow, a great personal sorrow, but at least it didn't affect the whole world. It was a world at war — but still it had no resemblance to what Mik was going through now. The end of the world! Nobody ever thought about the end of the world, but now it was here. Now it might be here. It was an impossible thought.

He felt that he had some kind of obligation. He had to get back. It was simply imperative. He could feel a word welling up inside him: Witness! He was a witness, he had to give testimony! It sounded pretentious, but it felt true. He had an obligation — *they* had an obligation — in some way or other he just had to make sure they got home. He had gotten them lost, so he would also have to get them home. That was simple logic.

But what about the Shadow? They *couldn't* leave him in the lurch. Maybe he was sick, but it wasn't right that he should die. It wasn't right to seek out annihilation like that — poof, groink, all over.

The world had changed, there was no mistaking that. It wasn't as beautiful as the world Mik knew, or as beautiful as it could have been, but it did exist. Not as many birds, no flowers in the wheat fields, no ditches at the side of the road, a lot more ugly houses, terrible sounds in the sky and on the ground — but it *was* the world, and the sun was shining. The Shadow must feel this way about it too, and love it, though he always spoke in a sarcastic tone of voice and always seemed to be on guard. All at once Mik could see what he looked like: a clown! The whole getup could have been worn by a clown. But Lars Kaj was no clown; on the contrary, he was smart and knew a lot of things and a lot of words neither Niels nor Mik had ever heard of or knew how to use. He might be a little older than they were, but still: so experienced, so knowledgeable, so brave, and so — wild. It must be an extremely complex and *rich* world that had produced him, a world that was now apparently about to fall apart.

By a high box hedge on a corner, the Shadow stopped and pointed. Across the street on the other side of a square they could see a big S, which both Niels and Mik recognized. It must be an S-train station. Many people were streaming out of it, and several were carrying heavy suitcases and back-packs. All of them seemed to be in a hurry, and all of them were moving in the same direction: away from the city. It didn't look as if people were talking to each other. They were walking in small groups — mostly a father and mother with their children. There was no socializing — everything was directed toward one goal, family followed family, in between came even more lost-looking single people trudging mechanically along with burnt-out expressions. None of them gave the three boys a glance; they barely noticed their surroundings at all. A blackbird sang in a withered jasmine bush. No one heard it.

Lars Kaj motioned them on, and they started across the square against the flow, down toward the station. The sound of the steps of so many people echoed in the tunnel under the viaduct, and Mik recognized the sound. It was the same as in the cave — and now he knew where it came from. Not this sound alone, but the entire spectrum of sounds: the propless airplanes, the cars, the television, the radio voice, the footsteps under the concrete, a suppressed or stifled scream, a huge muttering, a whining, that spread across the sky in all directions. That's how it was in this world, that's how it sounded.

There were long rows of trains stopped between the platforms. The direction signs showed the names of the various destinations; there was also a train that said Copenhagen Central Station. Apparently there was no one to drive the trains. There was no one checking tickets either — what would the boys have shown? Mik noticed an automat by the entrance to the platform. Maybe it had something to do with the tickets. More trains arrived, the doors opened, and people streamed out. Then the trains just stood there with a slight electrical hum and an occasional gasp from the vacuum system.

A man in a boiler suit came walking down the platform toward them. It wasn't an ordinary boiler suit, more like some kind of protective uniform with wide pockets and a high collar. He was carrying a helmet with a transparent shield on it, and when Mik saw him, he thought he looked like Flash Gordon from the comic strip. He looked tired, though — Flash Gordon never did.

"What are you doing?" asked the man.

The Shadow squinted and looked at him. "We have to get to Copenhagen."

"There aren't any more trains. We're only going in to pick people up, and we're not taking any passengers along."

"My . . . our mother can't manage by herself. I promised to help her. We've been at summer camp." The words flowed from Lars Kaj's mouth. "We got a phone call. We have to go get her. It's a matter of life and death."

"What's wrong with your mother?"

"She's an invalid. She can't walk."

The man took a couple of steps. "Civil Defense has certainly taken care of her." Then he stopped and turned around. "The city has been evacuated. Didn't you know that?"

"Sure we did, but that's why we have to go. She can't manage. We can't leave our mother in the lurch. We got a phone call that said we had to come, no matter what!"

"Don't you think that your mother would prefer that you stayed here?"

Mik didn't know where he got it from, but he said, "It's not her legs. It's not just her legs . . ." He looked at the man. "My mother is about to die."

The words sounded quite convincing, and suddenly they hit him hard. There he stood, dishing out a fat lie, and it wasn't because he was a great actor that it sounded true. And was it true?

He gave Niels a long look; he looked more and more like a scarecrow. Not much left of his old elegance.

The man studied them for a moment. "OK," he said hesitantly, "there's plenty of room." He wiped his forehead with his free hand. "Only crazy people and kids are going that direction. And me, but that's because I have to." He turned around, and they followed him.

The trip to the city had entered its final phase, and neither Mik nor Niels had any idea what they were going to do there, or why they were going along. There was the two-kroner piece, of course. But who was going to buy coins now? Anyway, it didn't seem to matter. Everything was evidently free. The man hadn't asked them for their tickets. They were getting a free ride. That's how it must be when everything gradually becomes meaningless. It just didn't matter.

The man sent them into the compartment right behind the driver's cabin; then he vanished and they were alone. A train arrived at the opposite platform, far down the track, so far down that people had to jump down onto the tracks to get off. It all took place quite mechanically, and Mik thought about a caterpillar he had seen once, when ants suddenly crawled out by the hundreds — from the side, from holes, from the eyes and nose. Finally there was nothing left but an empty shell.

After a while their own train started moving with a jolt, built up speed, and fell into a rhythm. If it weren't for the fact that the train didn't stop at any of the stations, they might have been returning from an excursion or Sunday picnic. They stared out the window. While the train was still passing through the suburbs, you could hardly notice the difference in years; everything was the way it had always been. The afternoon sunlight fell across gables and façades; the sound of the wheels on the tracks, the slight rumble and the little clicks between the rail sections, all ran together in a feeling of familiarity and infinity. Sparrows flew up between two bushes and chirped excitedly, clothes hung by clothespins from a line between two poles, a fence glowed red, a tricycle stood waiting by a cellar door. You could actually imagine that someone was waiting at home — whether sick or well — but that there was someone there at least, a father or mother, a sister or brother, who had put the kettle on and maybe bought pastry or was now cooking dinner, which would be served on a white tablecloth with knives and forks and glasses and a pitcher of milk or water. Peaceful, ordinary, everyday.

The feeling didn't last. The closer they got to town, the more it changed. Mik stood halfway up in his seat, turned around and stared backwards. There was something he felt he ought to take with him out of all that was disappearing. Then it was too late; he sat back down again. From both sides new visual impressions were pressing in on him: concrete streets, apartment buildings that looked like skyscrapers, television antennas, billboards. He could imagine the sounds. Then he realized that they weren't there, that everything was quiet, that the city was silent.

8

Light coming through the frosted glass roof of the Central Station made columns of dust form shimmering patterns. People moved back and forth in mute aimlessness on the platforms; groups of Red Cross and Civil Defense people stood here and there, trying to establish some order. Gone were all the festive departure and arrival committees, the handkerchiefs waving, the shouts of hurrah.

They hurried out of the train compartment. The man in the boiler suit was nowhere to be seen, but people were rushing in and claiming the seats, sitting down and clutching their parcels and bags and suitcases. Several of them had on a lot more clothes than necessary for the time of year, as if they had to be able to get through several seasons and counted on staying away for some time. Almost all of them had the same expression on their faces: amazement and disbelief, as if someone had raised his hand suddenly to strike them, unexpected and brutal. It seemed unfair, mean, and appalling to the people being threatened — but at the same time they didn't know what to do about it, other than to get their feet moving and see about getting out of town.

With the Shadow three steps ahead, Mik and Niels reached the arrival hall. It looked familiar, except for the meeting and information centers set up all over, and for the first time in quite a while they saw both soldiers and policemen there. No one seemed to pay any attention to the boys; they might as well have been invisible. Everybody was busy with their own affairs.

On the square facing Bernstorffsgade, there were rows of buses waiting, but there was not a streetcar in sight. Maybe they had all gone to the end of the line so people could continue from there out of town.

They cut across the street and stood outside Tivoli. The gardens were closed, but someone had pushed the teller gate aside so you could walk right in. It was a crazy feeling to stand there now, but why shouldn't they go into Tivoli, as long as it was free all of a sudden and they didn't know what was going to happen anyway, or where they were supposed to go?

The Shadow was still marching in front, as though there was some kind of meaning and a plan to it all, and when they got inside the amusement park they saw that a lot had changed, but that it still looked familiar. There were buildings missing, and others had shot up in their place — maybe it was the trees and the flowers that maintained the old impression, even though new, taller buildings on both sides crowded up against the outer walls of the gardens, reflecting in the pools of the fountains. It was deserted the way it usually was early in the morning, although the clock on the Town Hall tower was approaching half past five. With their eyes closed they could imagine how it would have sounded if everything were normal: music coming from the little promenade pavilions, the putt-putt of the boats' compressed-air motors, the splashing of the windmill buckets by the Tunnel of Love, the porcelain smashing, the Tivoli Guard drilling, the screams of the passengers in the front cars of the roller coaster.

There was nothing, only the feeling that there was a huge lid or a down comforter that was slowly being pressed down over everything, a shutter being closed, a curtain falling.

They turned a corner and Lars Kaj stopped. Down a stairway by a group of slot machines stood two young men with a crowbar, smashing the glass of one machine after another. It didn't sound like they would notice anything else, they were so engrossed in their work. Glass shards and splintered sheet metal lay all around them on the concrete; when one of them had smashed a machine, the other would bend down and scrape up the money that rattled out of the coin box.

The Shadow wanted to go on, but his movement attracted the attention of the two young men. One of them turned and said something. The other raised the crowbar and grimaced.

"Get lost!" he yelled. "Go to hell!"

Without seeing whether they obeyed the order, he set to work with the crowbar again, and the rhythmic sound of metal being crushed and glass shattering followed them as they half ran, half walked in the direction of the exit to Vester Boulevard. Outside an ice-cream kiosk Niels came to a halt. The others slowed down.

"What is it?" asked the Shadow.

Niels pointed at the kiosk. It was full of chocolate and cookies, but no one was in it.

"Can't you wait? There are probably tons of candy stores."

Niels shook his head. He had a tendency to these sudden attacks of stubbornness. It had to be now.

Slowly they approached the empty stand. The image of the bakery in the country town was superimposed over it. For a moment Mik saw the bakery lady loom up behind the glass counter, then he blinked and she was gone. They looked left and right, but there was nobody, absolutely nobody around. Only a couple of sparrows hopping around, searching where there were usually crumbs and bits of ice-cream cones.

As they were stocking up on chocolate and stuffing it in their mouths at the same time, Mik noticed that the Shadow had turned pale. His face was the color of the asbestos on the back of the toaster up at the summer house. And there was blood on his sling.

The chocolate was making Mik feel sick. He wasn't used to eating so much.

"You're bleeding," he said to the Shadow.

Lars Kaj looked down. "It's nothing."

All at once his legs collapsed under him, and he slid slowly down onto the floor of the kiosk. A pigeon cooed outside.

Niels and Mik bent over him.

"What is it?" asked Niels anxiously. "Is something the matter?"

They both felt that if anything happened to the Shadow, they were goners. They had gotten through almost everything together, and if he was out of action, it would be all over.

Mik squatted down. "Is it your arm?"

The question was superfluous; Lars Kaj's arm was bleeding heavily through the torn-up shirt they had used as an emergency bandage. Mik knelt down and looked carefully at his arm. Above his shoulder joint there were stumps of the broken bone sticking out through the skin. He felt dizzy for a moment, then he forced his eyes open again. It was inconceivable that the Shadow had been able to hold out for so long; all the sudden movements in the wrong direction must have made the lesion worse. It was a compound fracture!

"We've got to find a doctor."

Lars Kaj shook his head and opened his eyes wide. They were swimming behind the powerful lenses of his glasses.

"Why waste time?" he whispered. "Let's go to a drug store."

"But you can't walk! You were just about to faint!" Niels' voice was shrill and anxious. He knew how important the Shadow was too.

Mik straightened up. "There's a pharmacy just down the street, on the corner."

"Bullshit," groaned the Shadow.

"No kidding, there's one at the corner of Vester Voldgade and Stormgade. We can run over there!"

"You're crazy." His annoyance made a little color come back into Lars Kaj's cheeks. "There isn't any pharmacy there, we'll have to go all the way down to Købmagergade. Fuck it, that's the way we have to go anyway."

"Where are we going?"

"Over to Hubert's. To my friend's place."

"Hubert?"

"Yeah, Hubert, goddamn it! He can help. He's the only one who can help."

"What if he's left town?" Niels had opened up a chocolate bar and sat eating it.

"Hubert? He ain't going nowhere. I'll take bets on that. Where the hell would he go? And why?" Lars Kaj had pushed himself up. "You *can't* run away," he said, almost to himself.

Mik flushed. "Then what is it we've been doing? What is it we've been doing the whole time?"

"The opposite." The Shadow stared at him defiantly. "Do you think I'm running away? Do you think I'd let myself be evacuated? What would I want to do that for?"

"Then what about us?"

" 'Then what about us? What about us?' Is that the only thing you can say? Why don't you take the initiative yourself? I sure as hell didn't ask you to come along."

"But you said yourself . . ."

The Shadow's hair was flaming red. His hat had slipped to the back of his head. Furrows formed around his mouth, and his eyes narrowed.

"I said we had a chance if we went to the city. A chance to get away from the pigs. That's all I said. I don't care if you want to play innocent or dumb, or whatever, you understand what's going on here. You heard it yourselves, you can see it, so what the hell do you think is happening? You think it's Christmas Eve, or that somebody suddenly gave us the key to wonderland? You think you can just walk into Tivoli any day of the week and eat yourself sick on chocolate without paying for it?"

The effort was wearing him out, and he sat motionless

again. Then he said, "You can't run away from anything." He turned his head and looked toward the shelf, which was filled with chocolate bars. Outside the pigeon was still cooing. The Town Hall bell chimed.

"Well, what now?" Niels stammered a little later. "So what are we going to do?"

He looked over at Mik as though he had replied. There was no answer. They sat there without hearing or speaking or seeing anything. If anyone had walked by outside, they wouldn't have noticed that someone was in the kiosk. No one came by.

Then Niels got up. He was pale, and his snakelike hair was quivering.

"I'm going to phone my mother and father!"

"Niels!"

"I'll call them up. Maybe they're home. Maybe they came back from the summer house. I'll call them!"

"But you can't!"

Niels' face flushed, and he stared at Mik. "Why can't I? They wouldn't desert me. Would your parents? Why don't you call *them* up? Maybe they're home. All you have to do is call . . ." He bent his head helplessly and stared at his hands.

Confusion seemed to be spreading in every direction, as if Niels too had been subjected to a broken limb, an accident, as if he had been injured so that his bones stuck out through his skin. Seven holes in your head! A cup of blood! Of course it was all lies and craziness — but the craziness couldn't be allowed to spread. Mik didn't understand what the Shadow said, not completely, or else he didn't want to admit it to himself. But he knew Niels, and now he was scared, because things were starting to get out of hand. He was just about to say: But it's 1988, they're all dead, they don't exist anymore, you can't call them up. Then the logic of the thought hit him with its enormity, and he had to prop himself up with one hand on the floor in order to keep from collapsing under the tidal wave of emotions now crashing over him.

"Where's that pharmacy?" he asked the Shadow. "Where is it?"

He got up. It was 1988. And if it *was* 1988, his father and mother . . . No, he didn't want to think the thought through to the end, he just couldn't.

Mik planted his feet firmly and tried to make his voice sound firm. "We'll help Lars Kaj to the pharmacy . . . and over to his friend's place. And then we'll go back."

Niels looked up at him, bewildered. "Back?"

"We'll go back, the same way we came."

Mik leaned over and stuck his hand in under the Shadow's good arm. "Can you make it, Lars Kaj?"

Mik could hear that his voice at that instant sounded a little like the Shadow's. He didn't let on, but it was strange that he was able to learn something new in this situation. He felt stronger.

They got the Shadow on his feet, left the kiosk and went out the exit of Tivoli, and for a moment Mik was confused that Hans Christian Andersen Boulevard lay in front of them, but when he saw at once that there was no pharmacy on the corner of Vester Voldgade and Stormgade, he gave up wondering. Everything else had changed, so why not this too?

The wide boulevard stretched deserted to the north; the obelisk in the middle of Dante's Plads stood forlorn, and the statues in front of the Glyptotek stared into the distance. An armored car came rolling toward them from the bridge; when they had crossed the street they saw it continue on without stopping. A line of shiny black cars drove out of the parliament buildings at Christiansborg as they walked by; the cars quickly disappeared around the statue of Absalon and up Købmagergade.

The boys saw their own reflections in the big display windows — the ones that weren't smashed, with mannequins, furniture, and clothing in a jumble. They didn't stop until they reached the pharmacy on the corner; it was barely recognizable. Here all the windows were smashed in, and after they stood for a moment looking at the wreckage, they could hear sounds coming from somewhere around the corner. It sounded like singing, or at least wailing. When they sneaked up to look, they saw that a shop or some kind of café had opened its doors to the street and moved tables and chairs out onto the pavement.

It didn't look like just café furniture — tables and chairs and sofas had been taken from the big display windows in the neighborhood, along with handbags and leather suitcases. A man was busy rigging up something that looked like loudspeakers, and there were pharmacy boxes and bottles everywhere. As they stood watching it all, music came out of the loudspeakers, again that mechanical, thumping electric music, like washboards on fire and a tube that makes a radio screech.

The pavement was shaking, and up on the facades of the buildings the panes of the open windows were rattling, and two couples who had been lying sprawled on a sofa got to their feet and started dancing to the music. One of the women laid her head back and raised her arms in the air and rolled her eyes, while the other couple soon gave up and tumbled over onto the furniture, where they lay as though they had been knocked out. It was shocking to see so many people at once in the deserted city — they seemed to be totally out of touch. Mik had the feeling that even if they asked them something, they wouldn't get a coherent answer. No one had wanted to talk to the boys for several hours now, except for the train man; everyone seemed distant, withdrawn into themselves, or else they had fled the city. The café people were still here, of course, but far away, in another world, as if their backs were turned.

"There isn't so much as a goddamn aspirin left," said the Shadow. "They emptied the pharmacy."

"Who are they?"

Lars Kaj tossed his head in contempt. "Them? Those are the dopers."

The boys didn't understand a thing.

"There's no use wasting your time on them. They just come to stare at each other — even on the day the world comes to an end."

He turned on his heel, and they followed him a little ways down the street past the smashed, empty pharmacy. It was incredible that the Shadow was still on his feet; they couldn't imagine what it was that had such a powerful attraction, what it was that meant so much to him that he kept on walking, even in the wrong direction. Anyway it had to be the wrong direction, since everyone else was leaving except for the weird characters in the café, and those who saw their chance to rob and steal in the empty city.

Mik had given up trying to make any sense of it in his own mind. He didn't know why he was walking around here, or where else he ought to be. It was impossible to get things to make sense; anyway, how could he, when he didn't have the slightest idea where he himself belonged? The world was reduced to Niels and Lars Kaj and this peculiar city, which he did recognize — yes, it was his city, but now it lay like a desert, a huge empty space, a stage set where the echo of people's voices and footsteps hung ghostlike in the air after they themselves had disappeared. The city was empty, almost empty, and a threat loomed over it like a huge, indescribable monster. It seemed to be standing there already behind the old façades and gables, crawling over the edge of the roofs, leaning down toward the empty windows and peeking in. It felt as though the city were holding its breath so hard that it was about to lose consciousness, out of fear of suddenly being sucked right up into the air and disappearing in space, and a longing to burrow into the earth and pull it up like a down comforter. Mik wanted everything at once, but he just followed along, taking one step at a time, doing what was normal and within the bounds of reason, although there was no such thing as reason in his situation.

They had turned down a street where there was a big furniture store on one corner and a travel bureau on the other. The street wasn't wide. The buildings crowded in a little from both sides; they were old and relatively narrow. When the boys stopped in front of an entryway, Mik noticed that there was a larger, more elegant building across the street behind them. It looked like a palace. The gate was shut, and a white flagpole stuck out like a reproachful index finger.

Then they were inside the darkness of the stairwell, and the sound of their steps on the stairs echoed against the wall. The Shadow pushed open a door, revealing a large room that stretched from one end of the building to the other. He stood in the doorway with the others waiting behind him. In one corner of the room a man was working at an easel. Apparently he hadn't heard them arrive; he continued working and didn't turn around, as if he and the brushes and the canvas were all that existed in the world. Paintings were hung all around the room, and more stood stacked against the walls. They all portrayed some kind of flowers — round, rotating faces or suns that shone out from a dark background, green or brown. They seemed to cancel out the darkness of the stairwell and the room to some degree. Perhaps the painter was trying to replace the sunlight, which had such a hard time penetrating the gloom, with the light in his own pictures.

"Hubert," said the Shadow.

There was a moment's pause, then the man at the easel turned around. He had a long beard, black with gray in it, that grew all the way up over his cheeks; his eyes shone like the suns he was standing there painting. His clothes hung loosely on him. When he saw the Shadow he raised his hands and stood with palette in one hand and brushes in the other as if to embrace him. Then the light in his face went out, and he dropped his hands. He turned away again.

"What are you doing here?"

There was a long pause before Lars Kaj replied. "I came—"

The painter stood with his back to them. "I thought you'd been put away." He turned around again and walked toward the door. "I never thought you'd come here," he said in another tone of voice. He stopped and looked them up and down. "Are you hurt? Is something wrong?" There was worry in his face, and grownup calm and concern. "But come in, come in." He motioned them in and was suddenly bustling around them. He laid the brushes and palette on the table.

"What about your mother, boy? What about Ursula?"

Lars Kaj sat down in a chair. He seemed to have given up all initiative, as if he no longer wanted to be the instigator of anything at all.

"And who are they?"

He stood leaning over Lars Kaj, examining his arm and cursing softly. "You've got to lie down, boy, we've got to fix this, we'll just have to fix you right up. Then you'll have to take off again. You can't stay here — that'd be crazy."

He looked at the others. "Where are you from? Why did you come to the city?"

Mik looked down at the floor. "He said . . . that we had to visit . . . you, sir."

"Me? But why?"

"He said that you would be here, sir, and help us."

The painter moved around quickly in the room. His clothes flapped around him, his movements were precise and confident, even though he looked like something in a dream. His black beard pointed the way for him.

"I can't help. I can only do little things. Nobody can help now. The devil takes care of his own, and the rest of us have to do the best we can."

He went and got bandages and stood with scissors in his hand. Then he cast a glance at Niels and Mik. He looked away again and pulled open the table drawer, taking out a syringe with a hypodermic needle and a length of rubber tubing. Next to the syringe lay a row of gray ampules; he took one and stuck the needle into it. Then he tied the rubber tubing around Lars Kaj's arm and tightened it. He shook his head and smiled. The Shadow smiled back, and they gazed at each other. Then the painter nodded.

"At least it's pure stuff now," he said, "pure and certified by the government. Pure as the driven snow."

He let the needle slip into the Shadow's arm and loosened the rubber tube a moment later. Then he stood with his eyes closed.

"What about you two?" he asked, turning to Mik and Niels.

They shook their heads politely. "No thank you."

"Well, then the old man himself will," he said.

The painter bowed politely to them and prepared the needle and the syringe and the ampules for himself. Lars Kaj had closed his eyes and lay there smiling. After a while he said, "Let's get going."

It sounded like a challenge for all kinds of things; it encompassed not only them and the room, but in a strange way the entire world and everything in it: So let's get going!

Hubert nodded and walked back and forth, humming. Across the street lay the dead palace with the formal windows and the white index finger. It looked as though it hadn't been occupied for years.

"So let's get going!" Was there anything to get going for,

and what was supposed to happen? Mik tried to slip into the humming mood, but he was outside of it, and although he could see that what was happening was good for Lars Kaj, his own giddy feelings were different, completely different from those he sensed in his friend and the painter. Mik knew that Niels felt foreign and left out; he did too. It occurred to him that the painter, this Hubert, was a person his mother would have warned him against when he was a child, and then it flashed through his mind: but he still *was* a child, and here he stood with a man like that in a strange apartment in a part of town he had never been in before, and the man was doing weird things, and his friend already lay unconscious on the sofa, and there had been a dog, two dogs! And a helicopter and a great darkness and a window and men in black, the worst was the helicopter, the way it crept up the pine trees, suddenly flipped over in the air, stood on its head a moment and then whirred like the knife in a meat grinder down through the branches and tree trunks and disappeared before it arose again as a ball of fire.

A voice from outside came in the open windows with its metallic echo: "Persons who have not yet found their way to checkpoint 18-X, this is your last chance. This is the last warning from Civil Defense. Last chance . . . warning signal . . . constant rising and falling tone from the sirens will sound in fifteen minutes. All official groups will then have left the capital region."

The sound faded away, only its echo sank between the façades. The painter had started whistling as he worked busily with scissors and compresses and bandages. Then he raised his head and looked at Niels and Mik. His eyes looked like the pictures again: flowers with light like the sun.

"Well, let's hear it. Tell me the whole story."

Mik didn't know what to say or how to begin. It was an impossible story, after all, and no one would ever believe it.

"Where do you come from?"

Mik got up his nerve. "A hole in the ground."

It seemed as if the Shadow's smile was reflected in the entire room, hovering on the ceiling, fluttering down over them like gossamer.

"I found a cave . . ."

Mik grew more excited and it became easier and easier to tell the story after he got going. Finally he told Hubert everything. The long story came tumbling out, not making sense at first, but then it picked up speed, and Niels interjected comments, and in the end scarcely a detail was missing.

The painter was finished with his work by the time Mik stopped talking. He straightened up and stood for a moment with his hand on Lars Kaj's forehead, who was asleep. Then he went over and straddled a chair with his arms leaning on the back of it. For a moment Mik was afraid that now he was going to start laughing — or yell at them — and then he saw that Hubert had a friendly smile on his face.

"1941," he said, "forty-seven years ago. That was a good summer, as far as I can recall. I must have been eleven, or maybe only ten. It was good weather, wasn't it?"

Mik nodded.

The painter looked up. "Do you know what happened then?"

"No," whispered Mik, "only a little."

Hubert pointed to a shelf above a bookcase. "Go get that book. There are lots of pictures in it."

Mik hesitated a moment, then he went over and took down the book, which was big and heavy. The painter stood up, and he went with Niels and Mik over to the table. Hubert opened the book and started leafing through it. Most of what they saw was confusing and incomprehensible, but some pictures burned into their minds. Niels pointed to one of them. His voice was shaky as he asked what it was. In the picture, living skeletons were walking around — or were they real skeletons that just looked like something else?

"Prisoners in concentration camps," said the painter.

He pointed at another picture nearby. Naked, terrified people standing in line.

"Jews waiting to be exterminated in the gas chamber."

The painter turned the pages faster, pointing, shifting his gaze.

"Mass graves in Bergen-Belsen, the ovens at Dachau, lampshades of human skin, torture implements, the gold teeth of the victims, their glasses, their hair, soap made from corpses, the ruins of Dresden, the atomic bomb over Hiroshima, radiation victims, the shadows of the dead on the pavement, the Korean War, the Vietnam War, starving children in Ethiopia, Cambodia, Bangladesh, boat people, hostages, Aldo Moro, Teheran, the Rome airport massacre, the bombing of Tripoli, the Chernobyl meltdown, the contras in Nicaragua . . ."

He slammed the book shut and turned away. The two boys stood there sadly; they could see his shoulders moving.

Was he crying? What now? The Shadow lay in his smiling unconsciousness, and the painter had turned away from them. Were they alone again now?

Then Mik remembered that the painter hadn't laughed or made fun of them when they told their story. He believed it! Maybe he wasn't like other grownups at all, and maybe that was why the Shadow absolutely had to visit him. Could he really help them, or, when all was said and done, was he a dangerous man? — as Mikkel's mother would have intimated, without really explaining why he was supposed to be so dangerous.

The shining eyes were turned toward them again.

"You have to go back," Hubert said firmly. He pointed at Lars Kaj. "I'll go get 'Bettina.' She's parked over on Hauser Plads — if nobody has commandeered her — and then we'll carry Little Kaj down together."

Little Kaj — was he called Little Kaj too? So he had three different names. They didn't know that before now; naturally no one would go around calling himself Little Kaj.

The painter was already on his way toward the door; then they heard the Shadow's voice. "It won't do any good. It won't change a fucking thing. You can't run away from it." His eyes were glazed and he lay flat on his back.

Hubert turned around. "What can't you run away from?"

"You're still here, aren't you? Shit, you didn't take off!"

"I'm going to now."

The Shadow tried to sit up, but fell back right away. "Yeah, but why?" he gasped.

Hubert pointed at Mik and Niels. "Shouldn't they have a chance?"

Lars Kaj shook his head without saying a word. In a minute he whispered, "Give me another shot, Hubert, do you hear me? Give me another shot."

The painter spoke softly. "You'll get it, don't worry, you'll get it. We just have to get going. It's high time. I'm quite aware that you — we — can't run away from it. We've come too far down."

He paced back and forth restlessly. "It's ourselves we can't run away from, Little Kaj. Can't you see that? And it doesn't really make that much difference. But the others! Take a look at them. Look at those two . . . those two babies, they're brand-new, those two boys."

He went over and stood between them. They stood facing the sofa where the Shadow lay.

"Three boys," said Hubert, "that's what you are."

Then he turned quickly and hurried down the stairs. It was quiet in the room; Lars Kaj had shut his eyes. Niels went over and stood beside him.

"Why don't you want to go?" he asked.

The Shadow looked at him with his dreamy gaze. "I don't think it'll do any good. Where would we go?"

"To the cave. We'll find the cave."

Little Kaj closed his eyes again. "The cave? What's the cave?"

Mik came closer. "It's a place we know. Maybe we can find it again." He looked uncertainly at Niels. They had looked for it, after all, but the cave was gone. Or had they just been afraid of the man and given up too soon?

"I'm tired," said Lars Kaj. "I think you ought to take off. I'll stay here."

"We're not going without you," said Mik. "You're the one . . . who saved us."

The Shadow tried to sit up again. This time he made it.

"I didn't save anybody. You *can't* save anybody. I did the opposite. I dragged you along here. Now it's too late!" Exhausted, he sank back.

Niels was staring out the window at the empty building across the street. "It wasn't real . . . until we met you." He turned toward Mik and laughed a little. "Before it was just seven holes in your head — or a cup of blood."

All at once they heard the sound of a car down on the street. The sound stood out because it was the only sound there was. A moment later Hubert appeared in the doorway. He went quickly over to the drawer in the table and fixed up one more shot. Then he treated Lars Kaj, as he had done before, and when he had packed the rest of the ampules and some more hypodermics into a box, he carefully lifted the Shadow from the sofa and made a sign to the others to come along. They just managed to take one more look around the room — the pictures were still hanging there, and the sunny flowers shone from all the walls.

Down on the street they got into the painter's car, which was yellow and glowed with the same intensity as his pictures. Niels sat in front and Mik took the back seat, where he sat with his arm around Lars Kaj. The Shadow's eyes were halfway open, and behind his thick glasses it looked like he was smiling. His hat was in his lap, and his red hair was sticking straight up in the air the way it always did, no matter what happened.

As they drove out of town to the north on a cement road,

the sirens began to wail. Mik remembered the first time he had heard that sound. It was New Year's Eve, 1939, and they were supposed to visit his grandma and grandpa. He was sitting down in the living room waiting for the others to get ready. Then the sound came, and he didn't know what it was; he just noticed that the rising and falling howl crept into him like a poisonous snake you have no defense against. He had felt that this unknown terror — he had an inkling of what it was, at least — would follow him to the end of his days, and he prayed that it wasn't true. His father and mother came in and explained it to him — and that it was just a test, that they had known it was going to happen but had forgotten to tell him. That only helped a little. If death has a sound, it has to be like that.

Now he sat in the painter's car with two other boys, and from every direction in the deserted city came the sound. It rose and fell above the roofs, it squeezed down between the houses, it bored into your eardrums, it was sucked up into your brain and turned into nausea in your stomach, a black nausea that was fear itself.

Mik knew that the end was near, but he had no clear idea of what form it would take. Pictures from the big book he had seen at Hubert's crept into his consciousness; words he had heard the past few hours flickered past. Then he felt the Shadow's body against his own and pulled him closer, protectively. It was a feeling he knew from his own experience, how good it felt to be cuddled, and now he was cuddling someone else.

They drove out the long, empty road, and as they got farther from town other vehicles began to appear, mostly official ones — a couple of ambulances, tanks, a police car. Driving the other way it was difficult to recognize the landscape — they had driven so fast too. Then Niels caught sight of a name they had seen before and pointed at it. Hubert continued a little farther up the concrete road, then he turned off, and five minutes later they were in the little town.

Here too the streets were deserted. There were many more vehicles parked than before, even some of the yellow buses the boys had seen in Copenhagen. A blackbird sat on a TV antenna singing. It was almost sunset.

They drove past the bakery and the bank, they passed the little square with the post office and the laundromat. It looked the same as it always had. Of course the window was on the wall around back, so they couldn't see that. Mik thought of the nice lady in the bakery who had given them the raspberry slices. God knows where she was now.

Niels directed the painter to the edge of the field, where the car stopped. They sat for a moment in silence and looked across the grain and the grass. The burial mounds lay a little way up the hill. The light was coming from behind them so that they were almost silhouetted in the rays of the setting sun. The field was empty; the angry man had gone home. Now he was sitting with his anger and waiting for something no one could imagine.

"What should we do?" asked Hubert.

Mik leaned forward a little. His arm was asleep from holding up the Shadow. "We'll go out and look for it."

"I think I know where it is." Niels had his determined look on his face. He looked as if he knew what he was talking about.

The two boys crawled out of the car and ran up the slope. The painter stayed behind with Lars Kaj.

They were running fast, and Niels kept heading in a certain direction as though he knew exactly where they were going.

"That's the one over there," he said, pointing at the third burial mound from the left.

"That one?"

"It's got to be that one!"

"Yeah, but we already looked there!"

"We'll look again." Niels' steps were firm and confident. He circled around the burial mound, where no opening could be seen.

"You couldn't see anything at the ruin either, when you found the cave, right?"

"Nope."

"So we'll just have to listen."

"Listen?"

"Didn't you listen to find the hole?"

"Yep."

"Well, we've got to try the same thing here. Hurry up, there isn't much time!"

Niels' hair had started to stick up, the snakelike curls were undulating, and lively shadows were coursing across his face. He got down on his knees, and Mik did the same next to him. They searched for cracks, a little rift, the tiniest hole.

Niels stiffened. "Listen!"

Mik listened with all his might, but he couldn't hear anything. The sound from the ruin had been violent, a

whooshing, rumbling, and roaring, a huge suppressed scream
that was finally released. Here everything was quiet. Then he
heard a little melody. It was a very tiny melody, quite frail,
flickering like a tallow candle you're afraid will go out. He
stared at Niels.

"What's that?"

"Music. Can't you hear it?"

"Yeah."

Mik listened again. Once in a while he could just catch the
melody. He thought he recognized it. It was an incredibly
long time ago he had last heard it or thought about it. With
his ear pressed against the grassy embankment he pursed his
lips and tried to whistle along. The melody wound its way
into his brain and called up an image he recognized. It was the
Strand Pavilion, they were dancing inside, girls and boys
dancing, young men and young women. Outside the summer
night was almost transparent. The light from the dance pavilion fell on Niels and Mik's faces.

> Down the road
> Into the blue
> Between the green hedges
> Walking with you

You could barely hear it, but there *was* a melody. It was
sweet, vanishing and coming back again, teasing them, they
recognized it, and it kept coming back. Without looking at
each other they started in digging. With their bare hands they
attacked the burial mound, and the more dirt they scraped
away the more distinct grew the melody. Of course it was still

quite faint, but there was no doubt they were on the right track. Now they were going home.

With a great exertion they managed to push a huge rock aside, and there was the hole. They could still hear the melody, but there were other sounds now too. Mik recognized the airplane and the dry sound of the machine-cannon, there were heavy marching feet, a thunder of rhythmic shouts. The melody played above it all, flaring up, vanishing, returning. There were no flames around the hole the way there were when they stepped out of it. Now it was black, and darkness flowed from it.

They looked at each other, and as they lay there all their surroundings turned to negative. What usually looked white was now black. In an instant their faces were transformed to black blotches, their hands, their knees, as though they were already turned to carbon. Then they heard a sound behind them that was hard to describe. If a giant had ripped continents apart it would have to sound something like that. If you amplified the sound of a breaking heart millions of times, the sound would have to remind you of what Niels and Mik heard now.

"The Shadow," yelled Mik, "the Shadow!"

They both got to their feet, turned around, and wanted to run, but it was impossible. They were frozen to the spot by the sight that spread across the sky. Around a vertical pillar of smoldering fire stretching many kilometers into the sky, roiling clouds of flame and chemical smoke were spreading, an avalanche feeding itself, snapping at the corners of the universe and wanting to devour and swallow everything around it.

Night and day were consuming each other, and the city

they had run around in photographed itself on their retinas like an enormous scream. Against this background they saw that the painter was on his way toward them with Lars Kaj in his arms. He looked solemn and was walking slowly. Ten meters from them he stopped and carefully placed the boy on the ground. Then he turned around and went back in the direction he had come.

It was the wind that got them moving. They had forgotten that anything in the world could move or was really alive. Now the wind came like a roaring exhalation from the inside of a troll. At the first impact the firestorm knocked them down and they had to cling to the earth. Crawling half sideways, with their nails dug into the soil, they reached the Shadow, who lay with his eyes open, staring at the reflection of the explosion in his glasses.

As gingerly as they could, they took hold of his clothes and began dragging him toward the burial mound. He whispered something neither of them could hear. They lay down inside the opening of the cave, and as the grain started to burn they managed to pound the stone into place in the hole. The darkness closed around them.

Then Lars Kaj said in a clear voice, "What exactly are you doing with me?"

"We're going home."

"Home? In a black hole? What the hell is this?"

"It'll be light," said Niels, "if we can find the way. We have to get hold of the kite string."

The Shadow chuckled. "And the two-kroner piece. You never would let go of that. Shit, this is great — now it's a kite string. Yeah, that's just what we need!"

Mik moved in the dark.

"I'll find it . . . if I can."

He started feeling his way over the hard floor of the tunnel. The others stayed behind.

After a while the Shadow said, "Well, things can't get any worse, at least."

"No," said Niels.

"But if we tried . . . some other way . . ."

"Yeah."

Then they heard Mik's voice. It came from a long way off, but it was clear and distinct.

"I found it. I found it!"

Klaus Rifbjerg

B orn under fortuitous circumstances into a typical middle-class neighborhood south of Copenhagen on December 15, 1931 at 4:30 p.m., which according to superstition places me under the sign of Sagittarius. Both parents were teachers. Raised in security and confusion by two mothers: the one who stayed home to take care of me and the biological one who didn't show up until late in the afternoon. Two older sisters. After graduation from high school, a very encouraging trip to the U.S. as part of an exchange program, which took me to Princeton University in New Jersey, where I learned a lot about American literature and culture and how to mix dry martinis. Studies at the University of Copenhagen from 1951 to 1955, interrupted by marriage to Inge Gerner Andersen and just plain interrupted.

Début 1956 with the poetry collection *Under vejr med mig selv*. Critic for various Copenhagen newspapers. Editor of Denmark's most influential literary journal *Vindrosen* from 1959 to 1964. Tireless activity as a writer, which over the years has resulted in approximately 80 novels, poetry and short story collections, plays, film scripts, radio broadcasts, TV plays, etc. Member of the Danish Academy. Awarded the Academy's major prize, the Nordic Council Prize, etc. etc. Named Professor of Aesthetics in 1986. Literary Director of Gyldendal Publishing Company since 1984. Two daughters, one son. Still married to Inge.